The Visitor Series

The Visitor

Kids
Around

Book 5 by Dena Netherton

Write Integrity Press

The Visitor Kids Around
Copyright: ©2023 Dena Netherton

ISBN: 978-1-951602-15-4

Published by Pursued Books: an imprint of

 Write Integrity Press
PO Box 702852
Dallas, TX 75370

Printed in the United States of America.

Dedication

For Bruce, my faithful and true,
who works hard
so I can stay home and spin my stories.
Thank you, sweetheart!

Contents

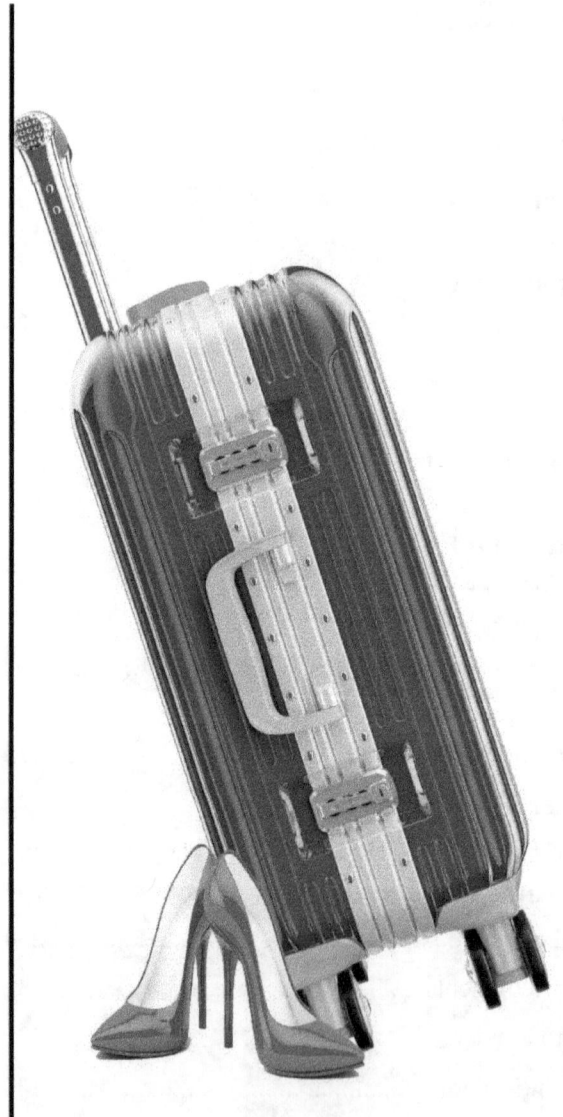

Chapter One

Life is Beautiful

Skye Wright jerked awake at the crash of breaking glass and a child's high-pitched shriek of terror. She jumped out of bed and threw on her robe. Was one of the children hurt? What had broken? Her heart pounded at the thought of one of her foster care children being injured.

She threw the bedroom door open. "What happened? Is everyone okay?"

Silence met her ears. She sucked in a deep breath and dashed down the hallway.

Samuel Fortier, her business partner and property caretaker, met her at the top of the stairs. He looked as disoriented as she felt. Could he have heard the crash from his cottage behind the foster care mansion? She cinched the sash on her robe tighter. "Sam?"

"I decided to check the doors to make sure they all had been bolted before heading to bed. Sounds like it came from one of the south rooms." His characteristic unruffled bass tone hid any emotion even though he raked his disheveled black hair away from his face.

Skye followed him down the hall, but before they could discover which room the crash had come from, a little girl bounded out of the Sea-Star bedroom sobbing then flung herself on Skye.

"What is it, Athena? Are you hurt?" Skye held the little girl, stroking her hair.

"My window! It broke, and now it's all over my bed." She looked over her shoulder as if fearing the shards of glass might follow her out into the hallway.

Samuel hurried inside to check the damage.

"I don't wanna go back there. Please, Miss Skye, can I stay with you tonight?" Athena buried her face in Skye's robe, her little body trembling as she continued to cry.

The door next to Sea-Star opened and nine-year-old Rocky stomped into the hall. "Sounds like some terrorists are after Athena." He folded his skinny arms across his chest and made a disgusted face. "Those guys are cowards, going after a little girl."

Athena cried even harder at the boy's words.

"Man, if they want to mess with someone, they should deal with me." The boy thrust out his chest and narrowed his eyes.

Sam stepped between Rocky and Athena, still huddled against Skye's waist. "Rocky, you should go back to bed. We've got it all under control."

Skye greatly appreciated his assistance. He knew how to handle the little boys and they never gave him any lip.

"Okay." Rocky slumped his shoulders. "But if ya need me, I got my lightsaber under my pillow."

"That's good to know, Rocky. Now, get some sleep." Samuel steered the little boy back into his bedroom.

Skye pressed Athena to her side. "Shhh, it's okay, Athena. You're safe. There aren't any bad guys out there, and no one's going to hurt you. Mr.

Sam will make sure of that."

Sam returned, holding his cell phone. He nodded toward Skye's bedroom at the other end of the long hallway. "Put Athena in your room and when she's settled down, meet me downstairs. I've already called the police. They should be here soon."

Just then, Mrs. Sally, Skye's most trusted night volunteer for the foster care home called Our Kids, emerged from around the darkened corner of the west wing. She had thrown an oversized sweatshirt over her pajamas and slipped on a pair of flip-flips. "I heard the crash," she whispered. "Sounds like someone threw a rock through a window. I looked out my window and saw a couple of shadows running down the road." Her eyes grew even larger, probably thinking about vandals.

The way Sally white-knuckled her sweatshirt collar, Skye could tell it would take a while to calm the woman down. Better give her something to do to keep her imagination from leaping off the cliff. "Would you mind making a pot of tea while we wait?"

Sally answered with a quick nod and headed

downstairs.

"C'mon, Athena. Let's get you all warm and cozy in my bed." Skye led the girl toward her room. Just before entering her bedroom, she turned and glimpsed Samuel checking on the children in the other bedrooms.

"There you go, sweetheart. Just climb under my sheets." Skye made her voice sound as soothing as possible. Once the girl settled in Skye's bed, she tucked her in and gave her a kiss on the forehead. "Let's pray."

Athena immediately shut her eyes and clasped her hands.

"Dear God, please help Athena feel calm and sleepy. Help us clean up the broken glass and let us all get a good night's sleep. Amen."

Skye hummed a lullaby while she waited for Athena to drift off. Within minutes, the six-year-old's breathing had slowed. Skye smiled down at the sleeping child. How wonderful it would be to have Athena's child-like sense of trust and dependence. They were qualities Skye had to work on daily to instill in her own heart.

She tiptoed out of the room.

Downstairs, Sam waited by the front door. Gravel crackled as red and blue lights, flashing through the side windows, alerted them to the arrival of the police. She left Sam to open the door for them and padded into the kitchen where Sally placed a steaming teapot on the table. Skye took some cookies from the cookie jar and arranged them on a plate.

In another minute, Sam entered the warm kitchen accompanied by a tall, intimidating police officer with steel gray hair and a handlebar mustache. "This is Detective Munson. His partner, Officer Ramsey, is outside checking things out."

The police officer acknowledged the two women with a nod. "Can you show me the bedroom?"

"Sure." Sam moved toward the entry hall. "It's upstairs."

He and the officer left the kitchen. Skye waited for them to clomp upstairs before speaking. "Sally, did you notice anything else about the people who ran off?"

The older woman slumped into a kitchen chair, then shook her head. "Whoever they were, they were fast. Two of them, I think. Running west toward the water." She bit into a cookie.

Skye joined Sally at the table. "Well, hopefully, it's just kids making trouble. I have a friend who lives in a nice condo complex. One night, some kids came through and smashed one of her windows in the kitchen. She freaked out, living alone. Turns out, other people in the area had experienced the same thing. They finally caught the kids." Skye poured herself a cup of tea. There wasn't much more she could say. Maybe the police officers would find something that would tell them more about the offenders and why they'd vandalized a much-loved foster care home that had been in existence for at least fifty years.

They sipped their tea for what seemed a long time. What could be taking Samuel and the officer so long to investigate one broken window?

At last, Sam and Detective Munson returned, this time accompanied by the other policer officer.

At Skye's questioning look, Detective Munson offered, "Probably just kids. We found foot tracks out back under the room with the broken window."

"And," the other officer added, "some graffiti

on the south wall."

"Could be some gang members," Samuel added as he glanced back and forth between the officers.

The officer shrugged. "We took photos of the damage, but I suggest you take your own so you can document the damage. In case it happens again. And for insurance purposes."

Sam nodded. "I'll take care of that first thing in the morning."

Skye stood, clutching the collar of her fleece robe. "You think it could happen again?"

Detective Munson grimaced. "You never can tell. Some kids like to target a specific house or business. But we'll make a report of this."

The two police officers headed for the front door and Sam followed them, his voice echoing back into the kitchen. "Thanks for coming so quickly."

Sally finished her tea. "Well, now that it's quiet again, I'm going to head on back to bed."

"Thanks for keeping me company." Skye gave the woman a warm smile while collecting the teapot and cookie plate. She waited until Sally's footsteps faded then rummaged through the odds and ends drawer for the flashlight. No way could she go back to sleep until she had inspected the south wall herself. And she wasn't about to wait until Sam's *first thing in the morning.*

"Where are you going?" Sam's voice communicated a certain sternness as he reentered the room. "You're not thinking of poking around outside by yourself at one-thirty in the morning, are you?"

Skye put her hand on her hip. "I won't be alone, poking around in the dark if you come with me. I want to see that graffiti."

He sighed. "Okay, I'll show you."

They stepped off the porch and rounded the building. Skye gasped, unprepared to find the large letters scrawled in orange reflective paint screaming, "Freaks. Go away."

"Oh!" She clapped her hand across her mouth. If it weren't for the neighbors, she would have yelled her outrage. Instead, she hissed between clenched teeth. "How awful. It's so cruel."

Sam slid a long lean arm around her shoulders. "It's not so bad. I can have that cleaned up first thing in the morning."

She blinked back her tears, especially since Samuel tried to encourage her. He always treated her with more concern than whatever had broken or fallen into disrepair.

"Why'd this have to happen now, with the fundraiser only a week away? Aunt Connie's arriving tomorrow. Now we have to deal with insurance and the window repair and trying to keep the kids from asking questions that we can't answer."

"One thing at a time, Skye. It's the way we've always operated." Sam bent and kissed the top of her head at a point just in front of her curly ponytail. Then he lifted a lock of her hair from her face that had escaped the rest and wrapped it around his fingers. "You should get some sleep. We can't have your pretty blonde hair turning gray. Things will look better in the morning."

Sam's kiss and the knowledge that he loved her and wanted to marry her brought her comfort. How could she ever operate successfully without him? He'd become her rock over the past year. The man who could fix anything, including a child's hurt heart. A man who feared nothing, yet could tenderly cradle a child, or teach the kids another praise song. Yes, she had business sense and a vision for the Our Kids Home, but it was Sam who made the kids laugh and gave them each a sense that everything would be all right.

"I certainly hope things are better tomorrow." She turned and headed for the front entrance.

"They will be." Sam's voice rang with confidence. "See you in the morning."

Chapter Two

Rocky

Rocky checked to make sure no one was near the kitchen, then poured a package of gelatin into the pitcher of fruit punch. He gave the concoction a quick stir and replaced the pitcher inside the refrigerator.

Just then, footsteps on the back porch alerted him to someone's presence. Rocky hurried back to the kitchen table and sat in front of his now-soggy bowl of Cheerios. Nothing would be more fun than being in the kitchen to watch the expressions on the faces of the other kids when Miss Skye or Mr. Sam went to pour them a cold drink. Miss Skye would try to pretend she didn't know who had played this prank, but she'd know. She always knew. She'd have a talk with him when the other kids weren't around. She'd say what she always said, "Rocky, I expect better things from you." Then she'd lean close and whisper as she gave him a hug. "Don't tell any of the other kids, but you're my favorite boy."

He loved it when she said that. It was worth having to do extra chores as punishment just to hear Miss Skye say it.

Mr. Sam came inside looking tired and sweaty. "Hey, Rocky, you're still eating breakfast? The other kids finished half an hour ago."

Rocky picked up his bowl and stood. "I'm done now." He carried it to the sink and dumped the cereal down the drain. "See ya."

Rocky skipped out the back door, headed for the playground. Better to get out of the kitchen quick in case Mr. Sam decided to pour himself a glass of the fruit punch he'd just messed with. He liked Mr. Sam almost as much as Miss Skye, but Mr. Sam's punishments lasted longer. And they were not fun. He hated weeding the garden. But even that wasn't as bad as cleaning the toilets.

Mr. Sam and Miss Skye had kept all the kids

inside for most of the morning doing crafts and other stuff Rocky had no use for. He couldn't wait to get outside to practice his soccer moves. The other kids didn't know why they had to stay inside. Even Athena just thought her window broke all by itself. Something else other than a tossed rock must have happened outside her window. Why else would Mr. Sam have taken all those cleaning supplies outside earlier in the morning and returned all sweaty?

He'd thrown enough rocks at windows—before he'd come to live at Our Kids—to know the fun in hearing the glass shatter. You had to run fast after that, before the person who lived in the house saw you. But somehow it didn't seem so fun thinking about some other kids—strangers—throwing rocks at Miss Skye's place. At *his* place. Man, if he'd had a rock last night, he'd a blasted those bad guys.

Skye checked her cell phone for the fifth time in less than an hour. On her way from SeaTac Airport, Aunt Connie would arrive any minute.

Sam, bless his soul, agreed to assist the kids with their daily Bible lesson, leaving her free to await Aunt Connie's arrival and to take her out to lunch at their favorite sandwich spot down by the water.

At last, a snazzy fire engine red Mustang pulled up next to the front entrance of Our Kids. Skye hurried outside to greet her favorite aunt. "Nice rental."

Connie B. Wright's signature red pumps exited the vehicle first, then the rest of her, smartly dressed as always. With her usual high energy, she wrapped Skye in a firm hug. Then she gazed into Skye's face with her vivid green eyes before scanning the property.

"It looks even better than last year." Connie pointed at the planters on the porch next to the new porch swing. They, along with the hanging baskets overflowed with colorful flowers.

"Just wait till I give you a tour of the inside. Sam and I have been painting and remodeling some of the bathrooms. And, of course, the kids helped out."

"I'm sure." Connie winked with a giggle that

communicated volumes. "Kids can be so very *helpful* whenever a can of paint and brushes are within reach, right?"

Skye chuckled. "Are you sure you won't stay with me this week? I could give you my bed, and I'll sleep on the roll-away bed."

"Oh, honey, that's so sweet of you." Connie grabbed Skye and gave her another affectionate squeeze. "But you know me, sometimes I work on my computer late at night, and I don't want to keep you up. I've reserved the same room at The Sound Inn and Spa as last year, the one with the incredible views of the islands."

Skye tried not to show her disappointment. She relished times spent with Aunt Connie. Her enthusiasm always lifted Skye's spirits.

Connie gestured toward the passenger door. "Hop in and let's do lunch. Seaport Soups and Sandwiches, right?"

"Naturally."

After Skye fastened her seatbelt, Connie shot her niece a big, almost conspiratorial smile. "This whole week is going to be such fun."

Skye loved her aunt's confidence. Having her

around almost made her forget the ugliness of last night. Not to mention the lump of worry in her throat over the other issues from the past month.

Within minutes, they had parked and found the perfect table on the covered veranda overlooking the town of Covington's quaint and charming seaport. The morning mist had rolled away revealing the sharp outlines of Mt. Pickett and Mt. Constitution on Orcas Island miles to the west.

Connie ordered a double-shot espresso with her meal. The tuna sandwich on toasted rye with sprouts, avocado, and special imported Havarti cheese sounded delicious, but Skye settled for a side salad, and smoked ham with provolone on whole wheat. And she stuck with her customary decaf mocha latte.

As soon as their orders arrived, Connie leaned forward with an earnest expression. "Okay, out with it. Something's bothering you and I'm not going to eat this scrumptious food until you tell me what's up. You and Sam are okay, aren't you?"

Skye exhaled and attempted to show her aunt an upbeat smile. Thoughts of Sam always made her smile. "He's amazing. I truly don't know what I'd do without him."

"And?" Her aunt lifted one eyebrow and picked up a carrot stick that decorated her plate. "Any chance you might be getting one of these anytime soon?"

At first Skye didn't connect, then she lifted her gaze to the sky for a moment. *A carat.* "Cute."

"Well?" Aunt Connie took a noisy bite of the crisp veggie.

"I'm just not certain that I'm ready." Aunt Connie, of all people, should appreciate that. "Maybe I'm supposed to be single like you?" It was truly one of her greatest fears to say yes to something permanent when she should have said no.

Aunt Connie took on a reflective expression. "I'm happily single because the Lord has never brought His man into my life. Not for marriage purposes anyway. Can you say the same?"

Skye couldn't answer that. Sam was definitely the Lord's man. And he was devoted to her. Plus, he was amazing. So why did she feel the need to hang back?

"All right, way too heavy for such a gorgeous day. So, what does have your sassy little eyebrows all crimped together?"

Skye braced herself, trying to summon the courage to admit her difficulties. What would Aunt Connie think when she told her about this year's challenges?

"Oh, Aunt Connie, I've been trying to work things out before you arrived, but it just keeps getting worse and worse." Her throat tightened as she fought to keep her voice steady.

Connie leaned closer and squeezed Skye's hand, her eyes filled with tenderness. "Dear, you just tell me everything and together we'll make it all better."

Her kindness and reassuring voice gave Skye the courage to speak. "It's our finances. One of our biggest supporters is going through their own financial challenges and they wrote me last month to inform me they would have to discontinue their support." She looked up to meet her aunt's face. "We were already struggling with the costs of operations rising."

Connie shook her head. "But you're having a fundraiser next week. Surely, that'll bring in enough to cover your shortfall."

"I don't know." Skye pushed her salad around with her fork. "It's going to be close. And if it's hard to make ends meet this year, I wonder what next year will be like. Some of our board members are already suggesting that I try to find a cheaper place, maybe in another town."

Connie gasped at Skye's words. "But Our Kids has always been in Covington. Everybody in town knows you and supports what you do."

Everybody? "Do you really think so?"

Connie's elegant eyebrows pinched together. "We've been doing these fundraisers for years, well before you took over running the place. We always get a great response from the community and the local churches. So far, each year we've brought in thousands more in donations than is projected. What makes you doubt that this year?"

Skye left her sandwich untouched. "That one church who pulled out of funding us? Their contribution equaled almost a quarter of our budget. How am I going to make up that much? And at this late date?"

"If God wants you here, you'll get enough for this year. And the next year, and the next, and the next." Connie held Skye's gaze as she smiled. "He knows what your needs are. He loves those children, and He loves you and Sam, and the board members, and all the volunteers. Pray on this. Cast your cares on the Lord. Then wait and see what He does."

Skye's heart soared to hear her aunt's confidence, not only in her, but in God. Skye felt like the Apostle Peter. When she kept her eyes on the Lord, she walked—just like Peter— on top of the roiling sea of uncertainty. But when she took her eyes off Him and looked down, well, her feet and her legs, and anything else attached to her, were sure to get very, very wet with doubt.

She took her first bite of her ham sandwich. The flavors of ham and cheese and all the fixings thudded like a rock in her stomach as she pictured the awful graffiti hatefully scrawled on the walls of Our Kids. Who could want them gone? She doubted it to be merely a teenaged prank as the detective had suggested. The words indicated a more sinister motive.

Skye took a decisive breath. She wouldn't think any more on this while having lunch. Today belonged to Aunt Connie. She gazed out the window at the harbor. Little boats bobbed in the water, while farther out, sailboats glided north and south. The sun sparkled like diamonds on the calm waves. *Ugh.* Thanks to Aunt Connie, she had diamonds on the brain. When the time came, she hoped the Lord would guide her heart.

But here in this peaceful place, upbeat music played through the speakers on the porch. Sam liked it here, too.

Even danger seemed far away. Perhaps that rock through the window and the graffiti were just an isolated incident.

She'd keep it to herself for now. No need to alarm Connie about what happened last night.

Chapter Three

Saboteur

Skye headed toward the front door to see if Sam had gotten back from his morning jog. But when she opened the door, a woman standing with her back to the door startled her.

"Hello?" she greeted the unfamiliar back.

The woman whirled around, presenting a face that Skye did indeed recognize, and looking equally surprised. "Oh, hello, Miss Wright."

"Good morning, Ms. Devlin." Skye hadn't seen the woman since she'd first come to discuss volunteering or maybe fostering a child—over six months ago. That happened. People got excited about the prospect of fostering or simply volunteering. Then they would realize what all that would entail and reconsider.

Skye hadn't heard from over a hundred different people who had at one time been sure they should begin working with Our Kids. Kate Devlin was one of them.

The woman glanced over her shoulder again. "I'm sorry. There was a young man up here when I pulled in. He darted off that way." She pointed to the other side of the house.

Skye passed her and leaned over the porch rail, but she saw no one. Surely the rock thrower hadn't returned. Not in broad daylight.

"I just stopped by. I know that it's been a while." The woman's lips spread into somewhat of an awkward smile.

Skye remembered her visit a couple of months ago. She seemed terribly lonely even then and Skye had been surprised that she hadn't heard from her again.

"I've had some time open in my schedule, and . . . well, I know it's kind of late in the planning, but I came here to offer my services for your fundraiser. Do you have enough volunteers?

Anything I can do?"

Skye shrugged. "We have all of our spots covered and then some." The tall, elegant woman wore a brilliant diamond necklace that caught Skye's eye for a moment." There she went thinking about sparkling stones again. She refocused on the woman's awkward smile. "But we're always looking for more prayer support."

"Oh, yes. That's definitely something I can do. Her smile relaxed slightly. "Well, just call me if you find you need anything else."

"I will. Thank you, Ms. Devlin."

The woman turned then started down the porch steps.

The front gate screeched, interrupting the woman's words. Sam—in his running gear—jogged through the gate, letting it bang behind him. "Oh, hi, Ms. Devlin." He came to a stop in front of her and grinned. "Fine day for a jog, don't you think?"

The woman blinked several times, her face going blank for a second. "Uh, it-it's a nice day." Then, she turned and brushed past Sam, the rapid click of her high heels emphasizing an obvious need for haste.

A few seconds later, her BMW roared to life, and she edged out of the parking area onto 14th Avenue.

Sam waved at the retreating car and then faced Skye. His pleasant face torqued. "Was it something I said?"

Skye laughed. "She's quite a busy woman. It was so nice of her to volunteer to help with the fundraiser. I kept thinking that I'd hear from her that she was ready to begin fostering a child."

"Is that what she wanted?" He picked up a hand towel that he'd likely left draping on the porch railing and wiped it over his face and dark hair.

"No, she didn't mention the fostering at all. I was a little surprised. But she did offer to help at the fair. Only, we have everything covered a couple deep, thank the Lord. I asked her to pray for us. Maybe she'd be willing to make a donation."

"Not a bad idea," Sam came close and leaned down for a quick peck on her cheek.

She gave him a sidelong look. "That's your good morning?"

He pulled the collar of his faded Our Kids tee shirt away from his glistening throat. "Sweaty. I'll make it up to you later." He turned and moved toward the path that led to what used to be the gatehouse behind the mansion. Our Kids had once been a regal estate, and now the gatehouse had been remodeled to become Sam's apartment. "Don't forget that I'm going to take the kids down to Avenue Park. Miss Emily packed a brunch for them."

"Good, I'm glad you're going early. It's bound to be a hot one today."

Covington usually offered mild summers with glorious cloudless views of the sound. The high hills that loomed over the seaport town charmed visitors and tourists with their emerald carpets of northwest cedars and Douglas fir. Herons nested near the tops of those trees. Bald eagles, too. Locals took their kayaks down to the shore to cast off into the fish-laden frigid waters.

But today, the afternoon temperature was forecasted to climb to a toasty 90 degrees and Skye's petunias were sure to droop. After she'd completed her computer work, she filled her watering can. She soaked the hanging petunia baskets until they dripped with overflow then snipped off the dead blooms. That's when she spied the corner of white paper.

Skye plucked the paper out of the foliage. An envelope? Who would place a letter in a spot guaranteed to be overwatered . . . or overlooked? Except by her. She turned the envelope over. No addressee. No return address, either. She stuffed it into her pocket with a shrug and finished watering her flower baskets.

Samuel and Rocky came out the front door carrying tools. "Thought we'd fix that fence post next to the baby maple tree."

"Great. How was the picnic?"

Rocky piped in before Same could answer. "It was so fun, Miss Skye. I found an old dead crab and chased the girls with it."

Skye couldn't help laughing with Rocky. Old dead crabs claimed the honor of being the worst of stinky things found around the shore. She could just imagine how the girls must have shrieked as they ran from Rocky.

"Miss Skye." He held up his trowel. I'm gonna dig a deep, deep hole."

"All the way to China?"

The boy's face scrunched. "Huh?"

Skye laughed again. "Never mind, Rocky. Just an old joke."

Sam and Rocky tromped down the porch steps, and Skye carried her watering can and the mysterious letter inside. Skye tore the envelope open as she walked into the kitchen but halted and gasped. Scrawled in juvenile lettering, the note read:

> To the bad lady who runs Ar Kids. Mov away. No one wants you heer. Even the kids.

Her stomach lurched at the mean words. She turned the light brown page over and found nothing on the back. The words bit at her again, looking odd on such a pretty piece of light-brown stationery with red scrollwork in the corner. What had she done to make someone hate her so much?

She slumped into a kitchen chair and read the

note again. Could this be a prank by one of her own foster kids? No, it couldn't be. The oldest child who lived here presently was a sweet fourteen-year-old girl named Claire. She loved to help cook and clean, and sometimes followed Skye around like a lost puppy when the younger kids had craft time. A note like this would have been totally out of character.

The next oldest child, Alex, had mental challenges. Besides, he was a perfect angel, always hugging her and saying, "I love you, Skye."

Then there was Rocky who obviously adored her. Still, he liked to play pranks. But his pranks amounted to things like hiding objects, putting gelatin in juice, or jumping out of dark doorways to scare one of the kids. He always tried to avoid anything close to reading or writing. The note didn't sound like Rocky's style, either.

She decided to show the note to Sam. He might have some insights she hadn't thought about.

Skye snitched a cookie from the plate set out for afternoon snack. But she chewed without tasting as she again read over the words. Who would want her gone? Who would think of her as *bad*? So bad that she needed to move away from Covington?

She shoved her fingers into her curly mop of hair then pressed them against her skull. She'd never had anything but the best relationships with everyone in town. And . . .

"Skye?"

She jumped at Sam's voice, then straightened her backbone.

"Sorry. I thought you heard me come in. Rocky says he'd like a cookie and a glass of water. I could use a snack, too." He set some cups and a plastic pitcher on the table. And grinned when she put a handful of cookies on a plate for them.

"How are they?" He said, eyeing the perfectly golden oatmeal cookies.

"What? Oh, the cookies? I don't know."

Sam slanted an eyebrow. "Didn't you just eat one?" He chuckled when she brushed crumbs from her lips.

"I-I guess I did eat a cookie. I'm a little distracted today."

He laid a gentle hand on her shoulder. "Talk tonight?"

She met his eyes, and nodded, loving how he never pressed her to explain until she was ready.

Yep, she would definitely unburden herself when they took their customary stroll after the kids went to bed and the volunteers settled in to be night-time supervisors.

Chapter Four

For a Few Dollars More

Connie showed up at the front door after dinnertime, holding a satchel with a you're-going-to-love-what-I-have-to-say smile of excitement on her face. "Skye, I think I might have found another supporter for Our Kids." She marched into the parlor and plunked the satchel on the coffee table. "Come sit with me."

A new donor? Skye had talked to just about everyone in town over the last few months, looking for additional supporters. If Connie found one on her first day in Covington, she had to be a miracle-worker. Before she could ask Connie the new prospective donor's name, her aunt pulled out some papers.

"Remember when we were doing last year's fundraiser? There was this pastor who had just been hired. Not in Covington, but east of here. In Skagit County. He said he was excited about Our Kids, and he thought he could persuade his elders and the congregation to get on board with supporting us."

"And?" Skye's heartrate accelerated.

"Well, I decided to give him a call. He said that a lot had changed, their church has grown, and now they were seriously ready to consider helping us with funds, maybe even provide some volunteers, too."

Skye clasped her hands to her heart. "So, have they decided?"

"Almost. They have their business meeting in a couple of weeks." Connie handed Skye the sheet of paper with information about the pastor's church. "This could be the answer to your problem."

"It-it looks great, Aunt Connie. But . . . uh . . . he didn't say how much their church would give, did he? I mean, if it's a small church . . ."

Connie held up her hand. "Don't worry. We'll know more in a couple of weeks. And don't worry about the amount, either. Remember what Philippians 4:19 says, 'And my God shall supply all your needs.' All of them. Not just a couple. And even more than the ones you actually know about."

Skye took a deep breath. That was definitely the Bible verse she needed to hear tonight, especially after the ugly things that had been happening in the past couple of days.

"Tomorrow, I'll help you call our volunteers for the fundraiser." Connie closed her satchel flap. "And I have some ideas for more booths. Have you gotten the final permission from the police department?"

"Yes, and they've agreed to have three patrol officers on the scene at the park the entire evening. And, in addition to our popcorn and cotton candy machines we have three food trucks that will come."

Connie clapped her hands and graced Skye with a girlish giggle. "This is going to be the best fundraiser we've ever had here. I talked to your cousin, Mac, and she's planning to fly in beforehand so she can help with the face painting. And didn't you say that Pastor Young is going to give the introduction about Our Kids?"

The head of the board was a kindly man held in high esteem here in Covington. "Yep, right before the band starts to play. And we've got some of the best door prizes you've ever seen. Plus, a raffle for an all-expense-paid two days and one night stay at The Green Bay on Whidbey."

"Ooo, I love that resort. They serve the best prime rib, and their eclairs are to die for. Too bad I can't enter the raffle."

"I know. Me too," Skye breathed out a long sigh. "Well, everything's coming together. Next Saturday's going to be a blast." And hopefully, the hateful messages she'd been receiving would stop, so she could concentrate on more positive things.

Skye helped put the children to bed, along with Sam, Mrs. Sally, and Kira, a new helper who had just joined Our Kids last month.

She still needed to get some paperwork done before she could settle in for the night, though. Sam caught up with her as she tiptoed downstairs.

"Aren't we going for our walk?"

Skye released an exhausted breath. "I totally forgot." She laid her hand on his elbow. "Sam, would you mind if we skip it for tonight? I've got a meeting with the board tomorrow and they'll want to see my spreadsheet."

"Anything I can help with?"

"Sure. You can read off the numbers I have to enter. That would speed things up a bit."

He followed her into the office.

An hour later, Skye locked the office door behind Sam. "Thanks for your help."

Before she could even turn toward her room, he caught her and pulled her into a tender embrace as he whispered into her ear. "Don't ever be afraid to ask for help with all the admin work you do."

She snuggled into his strong chest. "I know. It's just that I always think I should be like Aunt Connie. She's so independent and self-sufficient."

"You're you. And I love you just the way you are. And I love your golden hair and your sky-blue eyes and the dimples on your cheeks." He lifted her chin for a kiss. "Marry me?"

"Soon," she murmured. Why did she keep

putting him off? He asked her to marry him at least once a week, and she always answered with the same *soon*. Hopefully, someday she'd be ready to answer with a *yes*. If he didn't tire of asking her.

"Sleep tight." He released her and turned to lock up the front of the house before retiring to his gatehouse apartment.

Skye trudged upstairs toward her room, feeling brain-dead. It always amazed her how running a foster care facility stole her energy—not to mention the extra stress of putting together the annual fundraising event. Was she cut out to do this kind of work? Aunt Connie seemed energized by her constant go-go-go lifestyle. Too bad Skye couldn't muster the same drive.

She climbed into bed and shut her eyes. "Dear Lord, please help me to do all the things I need to get done. And please keep this place and the children safe from whoever is sending us such malicious messages. Amen."

But sometime later, loud music roused Skye from a dream. She glanced at her clock. How rude. Who could be driving around outside, blasting their music at two-thirty in the morning?

The music receded as the vehicle passed the mansion. But just as quickly, the music blared again when the vehicle returned. Wild laughter and shouts accompanied the music.

Skye jumped up and stared out the window. As the car passed on the street in front of her, a man's arm thrust itself out the window and two objects rocketed over the Our Kids fence onto the paved patio behind the mansion where the children often played or had snacks in good weather.

One object landed and shattered. Immediately, flames sprang up, catching the patio table's covering on fire. The other must have hit the brick walls of the building because she heard the crash of glass and saw the flare of white light rise to her window.

"Oh, my Lord!"

Chapter Five

The Big Heat

Skye set off the upstairs fire alarm, then grabbed her cell phone off her nightstand and dialed 911.

Seconds after her call, sirens told her the police and fire trucks would soon arrive.

Sam ran up the stairs to meet her. "Are you okay?"

"I'm fine," she panted, half from fear and half from outrage "We've got to get the kids outside."

Mrs. Sally came down the west wing, three children in tow, a forced calm plastered on her face.

Sam ran down the hall and checked each bedroom. Kate brought the east wing children forward.

Athena broke from the middle-aged woman and ran to Skye. "Miss Skye, I'm afraid." She clung to Skye and wouldn't let go. "I hate that fire alarm. It's so loud."

"Everything's fine, Athena. It's just a little fire outside. The firefighters will put it out."

Fourteen-year-old Claire touched Athena on the shoulder. "C'mon Athena, I'll carry you."

Athena immediately turned and raised her arms for Claire to lift her. The wide-eyed children and their caregivers walked quickly in orderly fashion down the stairs and out the front door. Even Rocky didn't try to take charge or offer to fight any *bad* people.

Skye and Sam checked each bedroom before coming outside themselves. As they joined the children and volunteers assembled on the sidewalk across the street, sirens blared. Amid the din, Sally took the rollcall to make sure all had escaped. Neighbors from across the street came out of their homes and surrounded the frightened children, trying to comfort them. Some of them had brought blankets to wrap around the smaller children.

Bright lights strobed through the front facing windows of Our Kids, mimicking the pounding of Skye's heart. The roar of two firetruck engines, an ambulance, and the police thundered to their rescue.

After the fire in the side yard had been fully doused and the firefighters had completed their investigation, a policeman that Skye recognized from the rock incident came forward. She waved him over. "Detective Munson."

He nodded. "Please instruct your volunteers to take the children back inside."

Skye found Mrs. Sally and told her what the officer said. When she returned, he took out a notebook. "Can you tell me what alerted you to the fire?"

Skye's mouth felt so dry she could hardly talk. "I woke up to a car driving by with really loud music. It drove by at least a couple of times. Then when it returned, I saw the passenger throw out two bottles. Into our yard. And when they shattered, they kind of exploded into a fire."

"Did you get a look at those in the car?"

Skye shook her head. "There were two of them, but it was too dark. All I saw was the guy's arm when he threw the bottles."

"Car? License?"

"Didn't see the license plate. B-but it was an older car. Loud motor . . . like the muffler needed to be replaced. Blue or black. Probably a Ford. Four-door. Sedan. Kind of beat up."

Officer Munson turned to Sam. "Mr. Fortier, did you see anything outside when the fire started?"

"Sorry, Officer. I heard the music, but I thought it was just some obnoxious driver trying to wake up the neighborhood. I only heard them pass by once, though. Guess I sleep a little more soundly. By the time I got to my window to look out, there was nothing there." Sam slipped his arm around Skye's shoulder. "I didn't even know there was a fire until I heard the alarm. Good thing Skye saw what happened."

"This question's for both of you. Since this is the second time this week you've had something dangerous happen here, I have to ask. Have you had any negative interactions with any of your neighbors lately?"

"No," they both answered.

Should Skye tell the man about the note she'd found?

"What about the businesses you deal with? An argument, or a misunderstanding? A disgruntled former employee or volunteer?"

Skye threw her hands up in a gesture of frustration and bewilderment "No one."

Sam's gaze swept over the attractive brick mansion. "We've been running Our Kids Foster Home for several years, and we've never had anything but friendly relationships with all the townspeople. As far as we know, all of Covington loves what we do and they're in full support of our operation."

Skye nodded, but the words she planned to add to Sam's caught in her throat. Had they made someone mad without realizing it?

Munson grunted and jotted a few more words into his notebook. "Sam, I believe you. But I suggest you try to remember your interactions within the past couple of months."

Sam shrugged. "Okay."

Officer Munson grimaced. "This isn't a case of vandalism anymore. This is arson."

"Arson!" Skye grasped Sam's hand. The warmth and strength of his grip immediately bolstered her.

"Lieutenant Calhoun of the Covington Fire Department told me that besides the shattered bottles, they found a liquid. They still have to do tests, but it looks like an accelerant was used. The way the fire spread so quickly, it's clear that the perpetrator was trying to do a lot of damage."

"Oh, my Lord." Skye clapped her hand up over her mouth. What had seemed worrisome for the past few days had now crossed over to dangerous and terrifying. How could she protect the kids from criminals when they didn't have a clue who was trying to hurt them? Or why.

She reeled and leaned for a moment on Sam before getting her feet firmly under her. She really didn't have a choice about keeping that note quiet. "Officer Munson, there's another thing. Yesterday, I found an envelope in the planter close to the front door. It was a message to me. Really nasty note."

Sam gasped. "You didn't tell me about this."

She sighed. "I know, I should have. I didn't want to worry you."

"Do you have the note?" Munson eyed her, keeping his face expressionless.

"It-it's in my bag. Inside."

Skye hurried back to the mansion to retrieve the note. When she returned, Detective Munson read the note, then read it again..

"Hmm," he said, as if mulling possibilities. "Looks like the top here was torn out off of something."

Skye stepped closer. Sure enough, there was a tiny, jagged edge near one corner.

Sam peered over the man's shoulder to also read the note, and his lean face settled into an expression of deep concern.

Skye mouthed, *I'm sorry*, then addressed the detective. "Do you think a child wrote it?" Or maybe the men driving around had pretended it was from a child for some twisted reason.

"Yes, maybe. Would you mind if I take this down to the station? Have some guys take a look at it?"

Sam spoke up, his usually calm demeanor visibly shaken. "Not at all. Is there anything else that we can do?"

She hated seeing how flustered he was.

"You guys keep your eyes and ears open. We'll add some more police drive-bys. And don't hesitate to call me if you think of anything more to add to what happened tonight." He handed Skye his business card, then turned to go.

But he halted and turned back toward them. "Oh, one more thing." He spoke in a quiet confidential tone. "Please keep the children indoors until you hear from me."

Stuck inside all day was like . . . like prison. It was prison.

Rocky wanted to get outside and practice more soccer, but at least he'd put his morning to good use. He stood back to eyeball his work. He had almost finished his death trap—a metal tray—filled with anything heavy he could find. Lots of metallic objects and some softball sized rocks, too. The edge of the tray was balanced on top of the window. He'd attached a rope around the tray to support it which fed into a pulley system on the ceiling. But when Rocky wanted to, he could unhook the end of the rope from its anchor nailed to the headboard of his bed. The rope would go slack. Then the heavy tray would collapse, spilling its objects onto the head of anyone stupid enough to try to break into Rocky's room.

"I gotta try it," he whispered to himself. He trotted over to his bed, never taking his eyes off the tray.

"Ok, bad guy's comin' up a ladder to my window. He's lookin' through, trying to find me. Ha! He sees me. He's opening my window. He's gonna get me. I'm waiting for him. The bad guy can see I'm real scared. He's smiling. He thinks he's gonna crunch me."

"You can't get me." Rocky unlatched the rope. The metal tray immediately upturned, dumping its contents with a crash.

"What's this?"

Rocky jumped at the sound of Mr. Sam's voice.

The tall man stood at Rocky's open door, surveying his dangerous operation. "Rocky, what are you trying to rig here?"

Rocky moved to the door and tried to close it, but Mr. Sam wasn't moving from his spot in the doorway. "It's nothin'." He grabbed hold of the slack rope and tried to pull it taut again. "It-it's just a kinda trap. You know, for the bad guys."

"What bad guys?" Mr. Sam looked more sad than mad.

"Well, you and Miss Skye are worried. And when the fire happened, I heard you and Miss Skye and that policeman talking. And the policeman said to keep the kids inside. So, I figured I could rig a trap to stop them next time they try to do somethin' bad."

Sam crossed the room and surveyed the work Rocky had done. He reached up and inspected the tray, then looked at all the spilled objects. "Rocky, this looks really dangerous. What if it came down on you or one of the other kids? Or what if it comes down and breaks your window?"

"Aw, I'd-a made sure no one I care about got hurt." He stomped over to his bed and slumped down onto it. Why'd Mr. Sam have to come right now? He had more work to do to make it dangerous. More metal stuff. It hadn't been enough to be really dangerous.

Sam crossed his arms across his chest. "I'm sorry, Rocky, but we're going to have to take down this contraption before someone gets hurt. I know you want to protect us, but let's let the police take care of any bad guys. And anyway, you're completely safe inside this big ol' house."

"Aw, man," Rocky groaned. Didn't Mr. Sam understand how important it was to protect the building from the bad guys?

A chuckle burst from Mr. Sam as he surveyed all the spilled objects. "I gotta hand it to you, though. You sure have a head for warfare. I wouldn't want you for an enemy." He sat down and hugged Rocky, still chuckling. "And you know what?"

"What?" Rocky still felt dejected despite Sam's comment. When would Sam stop seeing him as the sniveling little kid who arrived four years ago? Afterall, he was nine now.

"I think, when you grow up a bit more, our military could use you. You'd make a terrific general."

Rocky studied Mr. Sam's face. "For sure?" Did Mr. Sam really believe that, or was he just trying to make him feel better?

"Yep, no fooling." He hugged Rocky again, then stood. "Here, let me help you take down this stuff."

Chapter Six

Going to Blazes!

"So, I hear there were big doings last night." Connie settled into a chair at their favorite Wood's Coffee, a charming shop overlooking the Sound. "Firetrucks and policemen. Neighbors roused and kids scared. Skye, what happened?"

Skye stirred her Americano furiously, then glanced up at her aunt's kind face. "I think it's about time I came clean about our situation."

"I'll say."

"The night before you arrived, a kid—well, I'm not sure they were kids. Let's just say, some bad person threw a rock at one of our windows. Smashed the glass, scared one of our kids. When we came out to investigate, there was a nasty message scrawled on the brick walls."

"Oh, that's awful. Some people have no sense and no heart."

"Yes, and I had hoped that was the last of it. Maybe just some random mischief, that's it. Some gang members trying to scare us." Skye paused and took a cautious sip of her hot brew.

Connie leaned closer. "I have the feeling there's more."

"I tried to put it out of my mind. But then I found an envelope in one of the planters by the front door. The message said I should go away." Skye shook her head. Palpable frustration left a bitter taste that overrode her favorite blend. "Whoever wrote the note tried to make it look like it was a child's writing, but . . ."

"But?"

"Well, no kid pulled last night's activity. And I've seen lots of kids' writing. This didn't seem authentic. It looked like an adult had tried to disguise their identify. And of course, no one signed the note." She pressed her spine into the spindles of the chair and sighed.

"No, of course they wouldn't." Aunt Connie's brows knit together as she sipped again from her mug.

"I've been wracking my brain trying to think who would want me gone. I love this town and everyone I do business with. They're always saying how they love what we're doing at Our Kids. Lots of business owners tell me they're praying for us. And many of them contribute to our ministry on a monthly basis." Skye chugged a big swallow—too big—and choked a little on the coffee.

Connie waited until Skye had stopped coughing. "Sometimes there are people who just hate other people for no good reason. They've got hate in their hearts, and all it takes is one word to offend them. Or maybe you're too pretty. Or maybe you're successful, and they're not."

Skye set her cup down and pulled a tissue out of her purse to wipe her damp eyes. "I've gone over and over this. Remembering every place of business I've been to, every conversation I've had, even my relationships at church. And . . . nothing."

Connie reached for Skye's hand. "No one could be mad at you, Skye. You're one of the most gentle, giving people I know."

Coming from her successful and kindhearted aunt, the compliment meant a lot to Skye. She cast her gaze at the table. "And I've prayed about it, asking God to show me if I've been rude or insensitive. But, so far, He hasn't revealed anything to me."

"Because there isn't anything to be revealed, dear." Connie winked and pushed her apple strudel over to Skye's side of the table. "The strudel's marvelous. Here, take a bite or two while I give this some thought."

Skye took a reluctant bite, then brightened. "Pretty good."

"Didn't I say so?" Connie turned to watch a beautiful sailboat skim the waters nearby.

Skye knew her aunt well enough to know Connie could enjoy a passing yacht, barge, canoe, or kayak and still give her full focus to the difficult subject of who considered Skye an enemy. She took another bite of the strudel and waited.

"I've got it." Connie snapped her fingers, then whipped around to face Skye. "Here's what I'm going to do. While you're doing your final prep for the fair this Saturday, I'm going to go into each business along Cedar Avenue and get them talking about Our Kids. It's amazing what you can root out from what people say. And what they don't say."

Skye pursed her lips. "You're not going to ask them if they like me or not, are you?"

Connie sniffed. "Give me some credit. I know how to finesse a conversation."

"Sorry," Skye murmured. "I'm worried about alerting whoever hates me. I don't want this person to go underground for a while if you ask too many questions, then up the ante when you leave and really put the children in danger."

"Understood. Don't worry."

From her aunt's stern but quiet tone, Skye knew Connie had it under control. Relief soothed her troubled heart.

Connie shifted in her chair. "Now, about the fire. Did the detective or fire chief determine how it started?"

"It started up really fast because they used an accelerant, evidently. I called 911 and set off the alarm. The kids were excellent. They walked out of their rooms and got into an orderly line, just like in all of our fire drills. We took them across the street for safety and the neighbors came out and helped take care of them. Detective Munson said it definitely looked like arson."

"Oh, my word!" Connie's big green eyes grew even bigger.

"He said to keep the kids inside for a few days while they did some investigating. But I doubt they're going to be able to figure out who set the fire." And keeping all the kids inside when the weather was beautiful was like playing a Whack-a Mole game.

"Now I'm getting angry," Connie said, her voice sounding strained. "It's one thing to hate someone you're jealous of. But to put the kids in danger . . . Just awful!"

"I know." Skye shuddered, and shut her eyes, trying not to imagine how much worse the fire could have been if not for the quick response of the firefighters and the police.

"I gather the police will take measures to ensure your safety." She picked up her mug again. "And at the fair?"

"Yes, they have upped their patrols at night and

will provide extra policemen on Saturday. And we'll have lots of adult volunteers. So, I think we'll be in good shape. The event is going to be well-lit, and we have fences around the whole area. Sam has gotten some big guys from church to dress in costumes and they're going to patrol every inch of the festivities, too. And every small group from Our Kids is going to have at least one adult male volunteer as well as two other volunteers to be with them the whole evening."

Connie leaned back and sighed. "Sounds like you've got everything covered. Good for you."

Skye felt her cheeks warm. "I think so. I hope so."

Connie settled her handbag over her shoulder and stood. "I should be able to talk to at least half of your business contacts this afternoon. C'mon, I'll drop you off back home."

After Connie dropped her off in front of Our Kids, Skye stood and surveyed the lovely property.

She should have felt better, knowing Aunt Connie was fully apprised of her difficult and intimidating situation now and would be doing everything she could to figure out the mystery of the man or woman who hated her.

But even the sunshine, the gardens she had labored on for hours and hours so that the flowers and shrubs and trees would be a delight to the eyes, and the new information from Connie that Our Kids would soon have a new supporter to the ministry did little to lift her spirits. "Dear Lord, please let me rest in you. I know you are in control. Please help me."

Not much of a prayer. But sometimes the shortest prayers communicated the greatest urgency. She went inside and hung her purse on the hook just inside the kitchen.

Sam stood at the table, bent over a large bowl, up to his ears in flour and other ingredients.

When he looked up and saw the question in her eyes, he said, "Cookies for the Fair."

"Ah." But Skye couldn't help chuckling out loud.

"What's so funny? He glanced at her as he stirred the batter.

"You." She swiped a towel by the sink and came over. "You've got flour all over your face." She gently wiped the dust from his nose, forehead, and ear. "Where are the kids?"

"Kate and Mrs. Sally are doing an art project in the activity room." Sam straightened and smoothed his hair back. "Do I look presentable now, madam?"

She took the bowl from his hands and set it on the table. Then she wrapped her arms around him and rested her head against his chest. "You're perfect."

Sam slid his arms around her and hugged her tight. "How did your time with Connie go? I'll bet she came up with all sorts of ideas for figuring out who's giving us trouble."

"That she did. She's already down on Spruce Street, intent on doing some Jessica Fletcher investigations."

"Who?"

"Jessica Fletcher. Didn't you ever watch the TV show, *Murder She Wrote*?"

"Never heard of it. But then, when you grow up on a farm in Alaska, you kinda miss lots of TV shows. Besides, I find cows, sheep, and horses way more interesting than most stuff on television."

"I would have loved that. But, unfortunately, I'm a city girl." She released Sam and took a chair by the kitchen table. "Want me to help cut out the sugar cookies?"

"Nope, again. The kids are coming in here in about an hour to help me slice and decorate them." He gathered up the dough and rolled it into a long cylinder. "Gotta get this chilling in the fridge."

Skye stood to leave but Sam called her back. "Oh, I need to warn you about something else."

At her startled look, his voice lowered to a whisper, "No, it's not about our vandal. It's about Rocky."

"Rocky? What did he do now?"

"Seems Rocky overheard us talking to Detective Munson and now he's trying to get in the act to help us."

They sat at the table and faced each other. Whenever Rocky was concerned, the conversation took a long time.

"What did he do?" That boy was destined to greatness someday if his current creative antics were any indication.

"I was doing my rounds during quiet time and when I checked on Rocky, he was making a kind of contraption for stopping anyone trying to get through his window."

Sam's face told her Rocky's contraption wasn't all that serious. She felt her frown reverse into a smirk. "Go on."

"He'd managed to scrounge around and find some heavy tools and other things, piled them on a tray and arranged it so it would all come down on someone's head."

"Where did Rocky get all the stuff? He didn't take anything apart, did he?"

"No. Probably rummaged through those odds and ends we keep in the shed out back. That kid's so smart. His trap actually worked. I came in just when he'd deployed it for a test run." Sam shook his head. "Poor Rocky. He's such a little man, and he wants to help protect us all."

Skye's heart went mushy. "That boy," she sighed. "He's more of a handful than the rest of the kids combined. But I sure do love him."

"Well, the reason I'm telling you about his activities is I'm not sure he's through mounting his defense. So, we need to be extra vigilant. We need to check the garden frequently for any more traps. I'd hate for one of the other kids to get hurt as a result of his contraptions."

"For sure." She stood, feeling weary even though it was only early afternoon. "I've got some phone calls to make. Got some last-minute instructions for my fair volunteers. I'll be in the office." Tomorrow, her cousin, MacKenzie, would be arriving. She was practically identical to Aunt Connie, though fifteen years younger, and Skye couldn't wait to catch up on news from her about her upcoming wedding.

He stood, too. "I'll be here with the kids decorating the cookies. But later, if you need me, Sally and I'll be in the basement, rehearsing some of the music."

She watched him cross the room, loving the way his big boots made a manly sound on the hard wood floors. Somehow, it made her feel more secure.

Rocky didn't own a pocketknife, so he'd managed to swipe a paring knife from the kitchen when he snuck outside. He needed to carve the end of the sticks he'd collected from the big tree at the street-side end of the Our Kids property. Sally and Sam were in the kitchen with the other kids, but he did not want to decorate cookies. No way. That was girl stuff.

He set to carving his sticks to have wicked points on them. This would be the strike point of the swinging traps he planned to rig around the edges of the yard. Just like something he'd seen in a war movie. Except his were smaller. A bad guy just needed to step on the wooden footing, hidden in the grass. Then, the pressure of his shoe would release the pointed stake, lying flat. The stakes were attached to the footing with little hinges. Kind of like a mouse trap.

He didn't have time to put the traps together today. But he'd be back tomorrow to finish when he could sneak out again. For now, he could store his stakes in the shallow ditch behind the tree.

Then, tomorrow night after he'd placed his traps, he'd listen in bed for any scream of pain when one of the bad guys tried to come onto the property.

Ha. They'd think twice before they tried to hurt one of the kids. Or Miss Skye.

Chapter Seven

Suspicion

As soon as Aunt Connie came through the Our Kids front door, Skye pounced on her. "Well, what did you find out? Did any of the businesses have information?"

Connie held up her finger and tilted her head toward the door at the end of the hall. "Let's go into your office."

Once inside, Skye closed the door and took her seat across from Connie.

"I wasn't getting anywhere." Connie shrugged, and Skye immediately sighed in disappointment. But when Aunt Connie giggled, Skye perked up.

"But then I went into that dress shop, High

Society. Dottie's been working there for at least five years because she's helped me shop in that store many times. She was so happy to see me, and I just let her gab and gab while we looked at sweaters. I asked if they'd been busy lately and she rolled her eyes. 'Business is booming,' she said. You know how their clothing is upscale."

"Yes, mostly designer stuff. It's really lovely."

"Right, so they have some of the wealthier ladies in the area shop there. As Dottie put it, 'They're the ones who live up in the hills with the million-dollar views of the sound.' Most of them are really classy and polite."

"My, you sure got Dottie talking." Skye relaxed in her pivoting wooden chair. She shouldn't have doubted that when Connie goes to work, there's always a method to her madness.

"True. Plus, I found a yummy-looking sweater. It's a deep raspberry with gold and silver beads across the neckline. Ought to look perfect for the holidays."

"Aunt Connie!" Skye threw out her hands in a gesture of exasperation. "Did you find out anything?"

Connie raised her eyebrows in a teasing expression. "Even better. I witnessed something. As we were heading over to the changing rooms, this awful woman came in. Dottie sucked in her breath and said something about how she's always nasty with whoever's helping her. Rude. Snooty."

"Doesn't sound like anyone I know." How did this help?

Her aunt continued, "Dottie said that this woman flashed a big diamond ring around and spoke like she owned the place. Dottie got the feeling that she was some executive. She kept talking about big changes in the town like she was single-handedly going to transform the whole town."

"Oh?" Skye sat forward, and in her mind she again clicked through the ladies in town, wondering who it might be.

"I can't imagine why anyone would want to change this town. It's just about the most perfect place in the whole state of Washington."

"I can't imagine . . ." Skye gave up trying to identify the woman alone. "Who is she? Did you learn her name?"

"No. Dottie didn't mention it. I'm not sure she knew her."

"So why would you think this lady has anything to do with all our trouble?"

Aunt Connie shrugged. "You never know. I always get a little suspicious when people are unreasonably nasty. They are usually very angry, or have been deeply hurt, or afraid of not being treated with dignity. So, they push their weight around to force their control. Sad, though. They tend to defeat their own purpose. Whoever she is, she needs prayer."

"I agree." Skye jotted down some details about the unknown woman. "So, did you visit any of the other stores?"

"Oh, I made the rounds. But no one else was in a talking mood. For now. But as I said—"

"I'll be back," Skye finished her aunt's sentence in her best Terminator impression, and the two exchanged amused glances.

"So, what's the plan for tomorrow?" Skye gazed into her aunt's twinkling eyes.

"I've made a list of all the churches in the area that support Our Kids. I'm going to visit some of them. Try to connect with people on the missions committees."

Skye shrugged and twisted her mouth. That venture would be a waste of time.

Aunt Connie must have picked up her vibe. "I know what you're thinking, Skye. But sometimes you can find out some amazing information when you listen to the impressions of those who are deeply embedded in local churches."

"Just as long as you—"

"I know, I know, just as long as I don't insult someone with my line of questions." Connie's smile lit up her lovely face. "All I would like to do is have some cordial conversations where I tell the members how well Our Kids is getting along, how the kids are growing and maturing, and how we deeply appreciate their support. Then, if something comes up, we'll see."

A knock on the door made them both jump.

Skye cleared her throat. "Hello?"

The door opened slowly as if the person behind didn't want to disturb Skye. Sam's head emerged through the small space. "You've got a visitor. Someone you've been waiting to see."

Skye jumped up and glanced at her watch "Oh, my gosh, it must be MacKenzie. I totally lost track of the time."

Connie and Skye both hurried out of the office toward the front of the house.

Skye's cousin stood in the entry way hall, wearing a shy smile. She hadn't seen Mac in over a year, and it startled her how much she'd grown up to look like Aunt Connie. Same dark hair, pretty features, and fair complexion.

Skye opened her arms to her cousin. "Mac! I can't believe you're in Covington, finally. Remember how we always talked about the two of us living out here, getting an apartment together?"

Mac smiled. "It would have been nice. But now that I'm getting married . . . ."

"Yes, I want to hear all about your plans. Do you have photos of your dress? You're going to be such a beautiful bride."

Connie took her turn welcoming her niece. "How was your trip, dear?"

Mac grimaced. "Aunt Connie, I don't how you fly all the time. My flight was so bumpy. I couldn't wait for it to land. I tried to read my new book, to make the time pass quicker, but . . .

"Ooo, is that the book?" Connie asked, spying the corner of a paperback, peaking out of Mac's bag.

"Yep, and it's really good. *The Unsuspecting Heather Meyers*. Have you read it?"

"Not yet, but I will after the fair is over."

Skye lifted one of Mac's bags. "Here, let's get your luggage upstairs. You're staying with me."

Connie stopped Skye by putting her hand on her wrist. "Ladies, I'd love to hang out with you two tonight, but I've got a dinner date and I have to get back to my room to change."

"Who are you meeting?" Mac tilted her head.

"Oh, just someone," she said with a flip of her wrist and a teasing grin. "But we'll do lunch tomorrow, okay?"

They both answered, "Of course."

"See ya around noon?" Connie grabbed her handbag and hurried out the door. As soon as she was gone, Skye and Mac stared at each other.

"Well, that was a surprise." Mac giggled.

"I know. I didn't think Aunt Connie had any friends out here besides Sam and me. And did you hear the flirty way she said, 'just someone'?"

Mac shook her head. "As I've always said, 'Aunt Connie is layers deep.'"

They both laughed, then headed upstairs.

Chapter Eight

The Money Pit

The next morning, as Skye finished typing notes for all her volunteers, her cell rang. "Miss Wright?"

"Yes?"

"This is Rhonda Morelli from the Northshore Realty and Property Management. I have a potential buyer for your property. She had said you were considering putting the 1002 Seaview Heights property on the market."

Skye paused, temporarily unable to process this strange new information. "Uh, can you tell me who said I was considering selling?"

The voice on the line also hesitated. "Well, I'm

not at liberty to tell you about my client. But she seemed eager to make an offer."

Make an offer? "No one's come to tour the place as far as I know. And furthermore, her information that I was considering selling is incorrect."

"Oh, I'm sorry. Perhaps I'm a bit premature. But your property is prime real estate and if there's a chance you're going to put it on the market, I would appreciate it if you would let me know."

The nerve of this lady. She'd heard that realtors would sometimes cold-call homeowners of desirable homes to encourage them to sell, but she never thought she'd get such a call. "Ms. Morelli, thank you for phoning but I'm not in the market. If I ever decide to sell, I'll let you know."

"I'm sure my client is prepared to offer over asking price, if you think—"

"Thank you again. Goodbye." Skye tapped to end the call.

"Hmm. Strange." Wherever did this realtor get the idea she was going to sell her beloved Our Kids home? Yes, it was true that she struggled to pay the bills and wondered if a move to a cheaper area would help them operate with less financial concerns. But when had she mentioned these thoughts to anyone? Well, anyone besides Sam?

Skye raked her fingers through her curls. Who would want to buy Our Kids? And why? Was it someone who knew they were having financial struggles? Someone on the board? A pastor who had inside information? That would be highly unethical, but then again, even the insiders couldn't read her mind. Maybe Sam said something to someone?

The thought stirred suspicions she didn't want to entertain. Skye stood and moved to the window to watch the kids outside playing games with a big bouncy ball. Thankfully, they were allowed out of doors again.

Tears formed in her eyes. Why did she have to get this phone call, especially now, one day before their fundraiser? Now, she'd be looking at all her supporters at the fair with distrust. Was it Pastor Johnson who said she might sell Our Kids? Or one of the board members such as Lizzie Bender, or Joseph Strickland, or Ruth Dimer, or Dr. Palmer. They all knew finances were tight. But none of them had ever suggested she consider selling the old home.

What if one of them hoped to buy the home? A place like Our Kids could be transformed into a mansion for some rich person. Or, maybe this person hoped to flip the home into a fancy set of condos or business offices? The area surrounding Our Kids was mixed zoning. A coffee shop sat just around the corner. And a church stood two doors up in the opposite direction.

She hated to consider it. But what if one of her lovely board members wanted Our Kids for themselves? Would this person stoop to criminal acts to intimidate her to the point of selling their home?

Skye shook her head several times. No, it was preposterous. Too awful to consider. The board members were her friends. Friends of the highest caliber. Mature Christians who would lay down their lives for those they loved, which was anyone. No, she had to stop thinking about it. There had to be another answer to the mystery.

She almost hoped she'd get another nasty letter that she could hand over to the police. Or something like that. Anything that would help them discover the identity of the prankster—no—the criminal who was trying to scare her into selling her beloved Our Kids.

She needed to talk to Sam. Although she knew he would never share any of their personal financial business with anyone except the board president or the board treasurer, it was possible those two people had innocently shared Our Kid's financial challenges with others. Maybe he knew something.

Outside, Rocky glanced up at the window, saw her, and waved enthusiastically. She waved back and turned to leave the office. Time to read the little ones a story, and afterward, Language Arts.

But Aunt Connie's sudden appearance at her office door halted her.

"Do you have time to talk?" Her aunt hurried inside before waiting for an answer.

"I have a minute."

Connie took a seat and sucked in a deep breath as if she were out of breath, or excited, or both. "I just came from that coffee place on Harris Avenue."

"Harris Coffee?"

"Yes. I was talking to Molly, trying to get some info on some of her customers. She seems to know everybody."

"That she does."

"Do you have that note you found?" Aunt Connie slipped a sheet of paper from her purse.

"I gave it to the police. Why?" What did Harris Coffee have to do with that mean note?

"Does this look familiar?" Aunt Connie held out a light brown piece of paper with red lines and a little flourish in the bottom right corner.

"Where did you get this?" It was definitely the same paper. At least it sure looked like what she remembered.

"From Harris Coffee. They have some notepads that they order special." Aunt Connie pointed to the logo and the company name spread across the top of the sheet.

"That logo sure wasn't on the paper that I got." But the paper had been torn, according to the detective.

"I think you can be sure that someone had pretended to be a child when they wrote that note."

Skye nodded, and in truth felt a little relieved. "Harris Coffee is not exactly a family friendly atmosphere."

"No, more like modified office space."

"By day." Skye laid the sheet of paper on the desk and picked up the read-aloud book she intended to share. "By night, it's a gamers' hub."

"Have you thought about any reason someone might be pressuring you? Enemies? Anything?" Her aunt turned and leaned against the desk.

Pressure. The word hung in her mind. "You know, I just got a call from a real estate professional asking if I was ready to sell our property."

Connie's eyebrows rose. "What? Where in the world would she get that idea? Have you talked to anyone about selling Our Kids?"

"Of course not. I've never so much as hinted about selling. Sam and I have talked about what we could do if our finances got any worse. But we never talked to anyone else about this."

"That's mysterious," Connie murmured. She straightened, "Maybe someone has learned there's buried treasure somewhere on the grounds."

Skye chuckled. "If that were the case, Rocky would have found it by now." No doubt about that. "You want to stay for story time?"

Aunt Connie followed her out of the office.

"I've got some files from the Wright Foundation to evaluate and a few calls to make. Your Aunt Kimberly introduced me to a great connection last week when I was in Michigan. She might just come on board as one of our patrons. You never know."

Skye agreed. Good thing she relied on a God who knows all. She needed Him today. And she'd certainly need Him at the fair tomorrow, and all the days afterward.

Chapter Nine

Stage Fright

Skye settled into the comfy chair in the lower level of the house in front of her kids. "Today, I'm going to tell you a little story about some men in a storm."

As always, Claire had found a seat next to Athena so she could mother the little girl. Minnie, Athena's favorite friend, pulled a chair up to the other side of her. Alex half reclined on the couch near the back with his coloring book. Normally, Skye would have insisted that each child listen attentively to stories, but Alex seemed to be calmed by coloring. Two recent additions, a little boy of seven named Caleb, and his sister Quinn who was a year older, huddled close to each other. And Rocky, who liked story-time more than any other inside activity, sat smack dab in front, grinning at Skye.

"Now this is a true story. It actually happened. Long ago, some men decided to cross a big lake in their boat. It was a fishing boat for that is what some of these men did for a living. Their leader, a well-known teacher, whose name was Jesus, also went with them. He was tired from his long day of teaching and healing people of their illnesses. Soon, he fell asleep in the back of the boat."

Skye paused to turn the page and check on the children. Good. They were all listening. "Well, during their long ride across the lake, the wind began to blow. Then, it blew harder still."

"Like it does here?" Athena scratched her nose as she asked.

"Naw, this was a lake, not like here. This is the Pacific Ocean," Rocky said with a tone of impatience.

Claire spoke up. "It's not the ocean, Rocky. We live on the sound. A sound is a body of water that—"

Skye put her hand up to quiet the children. "Okay, let's talk about this briefly." She pointed to a map of Israel on the wall. "Do you see that big body of water? It's called the Sea of Galilee. It's more than just a little lake, like our Lake Paddan. This sea is very large. I know it looks little on the map, but it's about thirteen miles across. That's a lot of miles to row a boat. And when the wind blows across a flat area, like a lake, it can make your boat rock."

Rocky settled back into his chair, ignoring Claire's I-told-you-so look on her usually sweet face.

"Well, the wind got stronger and stronger, and clouds filled with rain came over the boat. The men tried to keep the boat still, but as the storm blew over, it threatened to swamp the boat and maybe make it sink."

Athena's eyes had grown big with fear. "Miss Skye, this is a scary story."

"Yes, Athena, it was a very scary time for those men. But they knew what they had to do. They went to their leader, Jesus, who was still asleep and shook him until he woke up. They said, 'Master, don't you care that we are about to drown?'"

"I'd be yelling at him." Rocky muttered.

"It's possible that they were yelling, Rocky." She turned the picture book around so the children could see the colorful illustrations. "After all, it was hard to hear during that awful storm. So, Jesus woke up and looked around him. He looked at the waves and the clouds. Then he looked at the frightened faces of the disciples. And you know what He said?"

Claire's hand shot up. "I know, I know!"

Skye called on Claire. "What did Jesus say?"

"He said, 'O ye of little faith.'"

Rocky frowned. "What's that mean?"

"Jesus was telling them that they needed to have confidence and trust in God instead of fearing that He would let their boat sink. And after Jesus said that, He spoke to the storm and said, "Stop blowing, stop raining, stop rocking the boat."

"And it did, didn't it?" Rocky had a look of discovery on his face which made Skye's heart melt.

"Yes, the storm went away. And those men in the boat, his disciples, looked at Jesus in amazement. Even the winds and rain listen to him." Skye shifted in her chair and turned the page to show the children the last illustration. "Do you think those men learned something about God that stormy day?"

All the kids nodded.

"Someone, tell me what they learned."

The new girl, Quinn, raised a timid hand. "I-I think that . . . that they learned they could trust God."

"Excellent answer, Quinn. I can tell you're a good listener. And I appreciate how all of you have been listening today." Skye grinned as she eyed each of them.

Rocky had been staring at Skye's book, so she handed it to him. "And now, it's time for Language Arts. All of you can move over to the table for today's lesson." She glanced over at Rocky, so brave and determined. He eyed the last illustration with something akin to wonder on his face.

Conviction pierced her own heart. How many times had she read that story in the Bible and thought she understood its intent? Now she rocked in a storm. Did she trust that God could keep her safe in the boat? And not just her, but her sweet foster children?

Just then, Sam came down the stairs with his teacher's lesson book. "How'd the story go?"

"Oh, just fine. Keep an eye on that new girl,

Quinn. She's a good thinker."

"Yes, I've already noticed. Her brother Caleb is pretty sharp, too."

Skye turned to go upstairs. The kids were already clamoring for Sam to tell them more about tomorrow's fair and what time they would be allowed to show up, and if they could get a double share of cotton candy, and if they could go into the petting corral to feed the baby goats.

"They're called kids." Claire's voice quieted the others.

"You mean like us?" Rocky gave her a mischievous look and let out a loud *bahhhh.*

Skye smiled at the sound of their sweet voices, their earnest questions and their innocence. They had no idea of the forces that threatened to overturn their secure boat. But she meant to keep them secure, trusting in the Lord and the loving adults who ran Our Kids.

Mac came downstairs, dressed in jeans and

working boots, similar to Skye's get-up. "Ready?"

"Yes." Skye held a hand to her midriff. "I'm all nervous, and I don't know why. I guess it's because of how many things could go wrong with the equipment, or volunteers not showing up, or . . . whatever."

Mac giggled. "Skye, you're still the worrier I grew up with. Everything's under control. You'll see."

"I know." Skye glanced toward her feet. "But, as Aunt Connie always tells me, 'Just be extra conscientious. Then you don't have to worry.'"

Mac grabbed her purse. "Well, have you been conscientious?"

Skye rolled her eyes. "Always." She slipped on her sweater. "My truck's in the back alley."

The grassy acres of park set aside for the fair were surrounded by mature oaks and maples. They would provide ample shade in the afternoon. Temporary cyclone fencing had been erected, surrounding the area. Skye had rented extra benches and picnic tables for resting and/or eating the hotdogs and hamburgers provided for their attendees. She and Mac set them out at angles to each other. They also set up tables to serve cookies, popcorn, and cotton candy, and other stations to provide ice water, lemonade, and iced tea.

At the far end of the space, a fence had been raised to contain the sheep, baby goats, and a miniature donkey for the petting zoo. Closer to the center, a dunking tank sat ready for its first volunteer. It would send several of the local pastors into the cold water. Some other volunteers would arrive tomorrow to paint the children's faces. Local artists had donated pottery, photographs, watercolors, and wool and alpaca items for sale to benefit Our Kids. Their booths lay ready and waiting for their goods.

Close up, a maze, constructed with bales of hale would keep families entertained—maybe even perplexed—for however long it took them to make their way to the exit. There were throw and toss contests with ample donated prizes to be awarded. For a door-prize, drawn at random from the tickets, Aunt Connie had arranged for the weekend getaway. And last, a band stand had been constructed for the music and the brief talks by Pastor Johnson, the board president, then Sam and her.

Skye and Mac walked the perimeter. "The kids are absolutely gonna love this." Mac gazed at the fairgrounds.

"I know." Little darts of excitement zipped down to Skye's toes as she took it all in. "Just thinking about how it's going to look tomorrow with all the volunteers in place, and the music and the food. I'm feeling like a little kid."

"Are you going to have a good crowd?"

Skye surveyed the area once more. "Oh, I think so. We always have a good crowd. The kids from all over practically drag their parents here. And we've been put on every local calendar. We've sent out tons of invitations and all the churches have announced it. Plus, we advertised on local radio, on our website, and all the social media. And all the businesses around here have put up our flyers in their windows" She let out a chuckle embedded in a sigh. "If that's not enough, I don't know."

"Then, you're all set." Mac wore a big smile. "I'm so glad I came out to help. My fingers have been itching all year to paint kids' faces."

"And you're so good at it too." Skye hugged her cousin. "Sam's going to be taking photos the whole time to put up on our website. Now, if the weather stays nice, the crowds will come."

Yes, the crowds will come. But, hopefully, no one to disrupt the fair.

Mac pulled out her phone, "My weather app says it's going to be warm and clear tomorrow."

Yes, Skye had also checked that app. But meteorologists could be wrong. *Stop it, Skye, you worry-wart. Trust God.*

Remembering story-time with the kids an hour earlier, she brightened. "I guess we're all set. Hey, let's go lunch at Guido's. It's right on the water and their lasagna is great. My treat."

They hurried back to Skye's truck.

Chapter Ten

Doctor in the House

Shortly after Skye arrived back home—before she could even hang up her jacket or her purse—the front doorbell rang. Never a dull moment at Our Kids.

She looked out the peep hole. A perky little man in a grey tweed suit came into view. Dr. Palmer. Now what could he be doing here, a day before the fundraiser? He had already volunteered to be their medical specialist in case someone needed help during the day. She sure hoped he wasn't going to back out with some excuse.

She opened the door. "Dr. Palmer, good to see you. Come on in."

Not one for much gabbing, the doctor nodded in greeting and followed her inside. He turned right and went into the spacious living area, pausing at the entry to let his eyes roam around the ceiling.

She'd never seen the doctor do that before on his numerous visits here for the board meetings or when he came to give the children their annual checkups and to administer their vaccinations. Now, he seemed more interested in the condition of the ceiling than getting to whatever he came here to talk about.

"So," Skye said, by way of helping him get to the point, "what can I do for you?"

"Oh, sorry," he blinked with a distracted air. He turned to face her. "I wanted to talk about where I can set up my medical station for the fair?"

"I've got that arranged for you. On the west side close to the petting zoo. We figured, if any of the kids got injured, that would be the best place. And we've set up a big tent with some tables and chairs inside. Plenty of room for treating a kid or two."

"Good, good," Dr. Palmer mumbled, still examining the room. "So, you think you'll get a large number of attendees?"

"Well, we've done all the advertising we usually do for our fairs." Was the doctor concerned about getting enough donations? Was he concerned about their last financial statement? Despite all of hers and Sam's assurances, maybe he believed their financial difficulty wouldn't be solved. "I've noticed that you seem interested in the condition of the living area ceiling. Is something wrong with it?"

The doctor seemed startled by her question. "No, no. One of our board members has noticed a slight crack in the ceiling, and he told me we would need to have it examined soon."

Skye brushed past Dr. Palmer and looked up. She was always nervous about the old mansion showing signs of wear. But scanning the ceiling, she didn't see anything worrisome.

She turned and studied the doctor's face, which she found unreadable. "Who noticed the crack?"

Dr. Palmer chuckled and gave a slight shrug. "Now that you ask me, I can't remember just who said that."

"Well, I'll ask Sam to have a look, and if he notices anything, he can get our fix-it guy in as soon as possible."

The doctor nodded.

"Oh, I have something for you. It's a map of the fair and where each of us will be stationed. I left the copies in the kitchen. Be right back."

But as Skye hurried toward the kitchen, the doctor followed right behind her. As she lifted a copy of the map and turned to give it to him, she hesitated. Doctor Palmer seemed to be examining this room, as well. Sudden anger tempted her to say something snarky. Although the mansion was a hundred years old, it had quality construction, and it was inspected annually by a certified county inspector. What did the doctor think he would discover that the expert hadn't?

She handed him the map, but instead of thanking her and heading to the front door—business concluded—he walked to the kitchen table and took a seat.

He bent to study the map, but she got the distinct impression he wasn't really looking at it. In a quiet voice, he said, "I heard that a real estate person called you. Are you thinking about selling the mansion?"

Skye felt as if she'd been slapped. He couldn't

have just *heard* about that. Someone had been leaking her secrets. And how dare the doctor bring this up, right before the annual fundraiser? Was he interested in buying the mansion? Why else would he be inquiring?

But when the doctor looked up, his face seemed kind and concerned. Or was he acting?

"I-I did get a call the other day, but I told the lady I wasn't interested in selling. That's all."

"Good." He stood up, folding the map so he could place it in his jacket pocket. "Thank you for doing these maps. I like to have a good picture of the way things are laid out."

She followed, still stunned that Doctor Palmer had heard about her business conversations. Who could have told him?

Her stomach had gone tense. So tense, she felt almost sick. She opened the front door and bid him goodbye. No sense in interrogating the good doctor and making him feel she didn't trust him. She stood at the door and watched him get into his Mercedes then pull out of the driveway.

Well, perhaps he had not been the gossip monger. Who then had shared her information?

Rocky checked on his booby-traps set up in strategic places around the edge of the yard. He'd rigged them so that the slightest pressure would trigger the swinging pieces of sharpened wood. To test them, he'd covered his leg with a potholder and stepped on one of the traps. Sure enough, the sharp stick flew forward and hit him. Hard. Without the potholder, it would have speared his leg. Good. Another layer of protection from the bad guys.

Rocky smiled as he gazed over the fence onto the sidewalk and street. A lady in a fur coat walked a little animal—he guessed it was a dog, but not a real dog 'cause it wasn't the kind that could protect you or scare anyone. It panted from trying to keep up with the fancy woman.

He jumped when she glared at him. "What are you looking at, street urchin?"

Rocky didn't know what an urchin was, but he wasn't in the street. "I ain't a street urchin, whatever that is."

She laughed, but it wasn't a sweet or happy laugh. "Just the kind of answer I'd expect from a little foster kid no one wants."

Her words felt like a mean jab in his stomach, and he wished he could lob a rock at her. "Lots of people want me."

"Oh, yeah?" She chuckled, like she didn't believe him. "How come I always see you here then? Well, it doesn't matter. You won't be here much longer."

She picked up her exhausted dog. "Come Muffy."

Rocky stared at her. She walked like a queen. But not a good queen. Skye would never be like that.

He needed to talk to her right now. She'd be able to tell him how he was loved and wanted. He turned and ran to the back door, but a truck engine started up at the side of the house where the garage doors were. Rocky switched directions and made it to the corner just as Miss Skye pulled the truck into the street.

He'd have to wait.

Chapter Eleven

Chase

Skye hopped into her car and headed down the hill for the supermarket. She had to get thank you cards for all her volunteers. And gift cards, too. She'd hand them out after the fair ended. Oh, and Sandi, her helper at the cookie counter, needed some more paper plates. At the market, the parking lot was almost full, so she had to squeeze her vehicle between two vans.

After filling her cart with additional items she hadn't realized she needed, she headed for the card aisle. Then she spied an attractive larger thank you card. This one would be perfect for Aunt Connie if the message inside matched the cover's uniqueness.

But just as she reached for the card, a movement to her right caught her attention. A man stood about ten paces away pretending to read a card. At least she figured he was pretending because the card was upside down. Skye's heart accelerated. Normally she wouldn't have given the man a second thought, but there was just something off about him. He appeared kind of scroungy. Unshaven. And his hair hung longish and scraggly. Besides, most men didn't buy thank you cards. That was mainly a woman's thing, right?

Had he been watching her? Or was she just getting paranoid? What if she moved to another aisle? Would he follow?

Skye pushed her cart down to the end of the card aisle. Oh, how she wished she could turn and see if the man still watched her. But she made herself amble, forcing her face to look unconcerned and oblivious.

The next aisle held office supplies. Nope, she wouldn't go down there. She had to go to an aisle more suited to women. Oh yes, toiletry and travel-sized fragrance sprays. It lay farther away, but if he showed up there it would confirm in her mind that he stalked her. Not too many men had an interest in cute little travel containers for creams and lotions. Skye parked her cart in front of a display of travel mirrors.

While she waited, she selected a mirror and held it up to the light as if checking her makeup. Sure enough, her patience was rewarded. If you could call it a reward. The tall, thin, guy came around the corner of her aisle. But as soon as he noticed her, he backed away. Skye furtively watched him through the mirror as a combination of fear and anger warred in her guts. The creep. He picked up some arthritis cream from the endcap. The guy appeared way too young for that kind of product.

When she turned back and hung up the mirror, he sidled over to be less visible. Good thing lots of people shopped in the store. And there were security cameras everywhere.

Skye pushed her cart to checkout. Even though she kept an eye out for him, she didn't see the man. Maybe he was just one of those creeps that liked to follow women around in a store. That had happened to her more than once at the mall south of town.

She paid for her groceries, glad she only needed

two plastic bags. With one more backward glance, Skye stepped outside. It had started to rain, and a blur of cars passed in front of the store entrance before she could proceed. The bags would fit in her passenger seat and keep her from having to get soaked to stow them in the back.

She glanced around again, wondering if the creep from inside had wandered in her direction again. *Take a breath, Skye.* It was just one creepy guy. She would be home in a few minutes. And just because he seemed grungy, didn't mean he was connected to all the things that had happened at Our Kids. Relax. She moved to the edge of the curb.

"Miss, can you spare some change?"

A man stepped forward. Tall and thin and scuzzy. The same one who'd been following her inside the store. He held out his hand. "Change? Change? Got some?" He came closer. When he opened his mouth, she expected broken or rotting teeth. But they were white and normal. Maybe even a little too white.

Maybe simply down on his luck, poor guy. How many men or women had she handed out free food to as they stood begging outside stores or restaurants? Many. And none had ever threatened her. *Get a grip, Skye.*

Clutching both her grocery bags and her purse to her chest, she tried to reach in for her wallet. But her fingers had gone fear-numb.

The man leaned over her. His eyes were normal too. No redness or glazed look to them as she'd seen in so many homeless men in the area. No, this man's eyes held intelligence and focus. She tried to speak, but her throat had turned into a desert. He leaned closer and his lips spread into a lust-filled grin.

Skye gasped and hunkered as if under the onslaught of a hurricane blast.

Then, in a panicked rush of fight or flight, her brain chose flight. Her legs exploded with strength. She straightened, brushed past the tall creep, and raced through the line of cars passing in front of the store. She found her voice halfway across the parking lot. "No! Leave me alone."

Heart racing, she sluiced through the rain. The spaces between parked cars seemed to narrow in front of her. She darted into the next lane only to get a honk from an oncoming car. She touched the hood with her fingers and held them up in an apology.

Looked over her shoulder. She didn't see the man but couldn't count on him not following. Not gaining on her.

She fled through the next gap, zigging when the car door in front of her suddenly opened. Narrowly avoiding an errant shopping cart, she finally reached her truck. She pressed the key fob, dashed the rest of the way, and flung the truck door open. Clutching her bags, she threw herself inside, slammed the door shut and locked it.

The sudden silence inside the cab shocked her badly as if a stranger from the back seat had tapped on her shoulder. The groceries, which had been clutched to her chest, avalanched onto her lap and down onto the floor.

But she sat alone.

She had heard on the news a few weeks ago about a woman getting to her car, arms loaded with bags and her purse. Not in Covington, but somewhere else in the state. A guy had hidden around the back of her car. When she opened her car door, he came out of nowhere and shoved her inside. Forced himself in, too. Drove off. The police never found her.

Other scenarios, a product of her nerve-wracked imagination, flashed through her mind. Skye's parched throat made it impossible to swallow. Her breath caught at the horrible image of the kidnapped woman. But the rough-looking man had not followed her. Cars pulled in and out of the parking lot. Rain splattered her windshield.

Skye sucked in a deep, shuddering breath. She needed to get home and recover from her fright. Have a cup of tea, put her feet up. And get a good night's rest to prepare for the festivities of the next day.

She pressed the starter button and checked to make sure it was safe to reverse. Good, a temporary lull in the busy supermarket traffic. Once out of the parking lot, she turned onto Perris Avenue, heading south. Yes, it would be nice to soak in a hot tub, then settle into bed with her mug of tea. Forget about the day's troubles and drift off into la-la land.

A car horn blared behind her. What? She was doing the speed limit, staying in her lane. Her lights were on. What then? The car behind her came up close, close enough to send an aggressive message. *Ok*. She sped up a little.

The vehicle behind her was still not satisfied. It came up on her bumper once again, laying on the horn. Her mouth went dry, and her heart pounded. She checked out the vehicle in her rearview mirror—as much as she could in the rain and gathering darkness. Not a police vehicle. No lights or sirens. Besides, what police officer would honk at another driver?

As badly as the rough-looking guy outside the supermarket had startled and intimidated her, this scenario scared her worse. She'd heard about people being forced to the side of the road by weird drivers.

Could this be a case of road-rage? But she hadn't done anything, not that it mattered. Some people got upset over nothing.

Skye turned on her signal and prepared to turn onto Betty Way. Hopefully the driver would keep going straight ahead.

But when she made the turn, he or she turned also. Skye fumbled in her purse for her cell phone. It was hard to drive down the narrow road and dial 911 at the same time. When the dispatcher answered, she sputtered, "There's a car following me. I don't know why. Acting crazy and mad."

She speeded up. "I don't know why, but he's acting like he wants to hurt me. Like he's angry or something."

Simpson Street came up on her right. This time she wouldn't signal. She'd turn quick, and maybe she'd lose the driver.

The dispatcher's calm voice asked for her location.

"I-I just turned onto Simpson, going uphill. I'm uh, driving a blue Dodge pickup."

Skye made another turn. Onto an unfamiliar street. "I, I, I don't know what street I'm on now. I'm way uphill. Close to the university. He's still following. Still honking. He's right on my tail."

She gasped when a dead-end sign appeared. Oh, no! She'd be trapped.

An empty driveway came up on her left. Skye screeched into the free space then backed out to head the way she'd come, nearly colliding with her pursuer. As she passed, the guy rolled down his window.

"You're in trouble, lady!" he yelled. Then he threw his head back and laughed as if he were riding a roller coaster and enjoying the ride.

Skye got a brief glimpse of the man. "Oh, my Lord, it's the weird guy."

She didn't mean for the dispatcher to hear her, but she did. Questions shot out of the phone, into Skye's ear. Describe the car. What make? Model?

"It's a dark color. Older. Bad muffler."

License? No, she couldn't make it out.

"I'm turning back onto Simpson, heading downhill. He's still behind me. Waving his arm out the window. Making rude gestures. No, I don't see a gun." She answered the battery of questions. "It's a Ford. Old. Maybe about 2000. It's dark blue. Sedan. Still can't see the license plate through the rain."

She didn't have a weapon, but Sam had taught her some really effective self-defense moves. Maybe she should pull over and get ready for a physical confrontation?

No, that's stupid. He was a wiry man and at least a foot taller than she was. Probably knew how to fight, too. And what if he was hiding a gun or knife?

Skye turned back onto Betty Way, going south. She wouldn't turn onto Coast Drive. Couldn't try to go home. What if he followed her all that way? She didn't want him to know where she lived. Or worse, force her inside and trap the children, too.

She turned west, heading to the police station. He wouldn't follow her there. "I'm heading to the police station. The one on Railroad. No, I can't stop. This guy is crazy. The way he's acting, he could knock out my window and drag me out of my truck."

Flashing lights up ahead alerted her. Was it in response to her call? Even if it wasn't, she'd flag down any officer coming her way. As soon as the speeding police vehicle got close, she flashed her lights several times, then pulled over. The police car immediately pulled in behind her.

Skye checked her rear view. Her pursuer had vanished.

The Visitor Kids Around

122

Chapter Twelve

First Blood

Through her open window, she explained what had happened to the police officer. The poor man was doused even though he wore a navy slicker, but she couldn't have looked much better after her run in the rain. And as it was, spray continued to blow through the open window into her face.

He directed her to follow him to the station to make out a full report of the incident.

Incident. That word made her harrowing experience seem dry, even boring. Like the time she had accidentally backed into a two-hour parking sign downtown and had called the police to let them know what she had done. They'd sent an officer who took her statement and then directed her to take her own photos of the damage and contact her insurance. Though the officer had been nice, her issue had been treated as ordinary and typical.

This situation was anything but ordinary and typical.

The policeman, Officer Stanton, led her into a small office and sat down across from her with a notepad. He listened with an impassive face as she told her story. But his voice was kind, and she could tell he felt bad for what she had just gone through.

"I'm going to call Samuel Fortier, my business partner, if that's okay.

"That's fine. I'll have your statement prepared for you." He left.

Sam didn't answer, so she texted him to let him know where she was. He would have to wait in the lobby anyway.

A young woman, carrying a laptop, entered and took a seat next to Skye.

"My name's Jill and I'll be composing your description of the man who followed you."

A few minutes later, Officer Stanton came back in, accompanied by Detective Munson. "Detective

Munson is familiar with your case, so we asked him to handle this interview."

At the sight of a familiar face, Skye almost cried in relief. But she reined in the impulse.

The detective sat down across from Skye. "Miss Wright, tell me about the man who followed you. Can you describe him?"

Skye took a deep breath, forcing her voice to stay even and quiet. "He's tall. And—"

"Hold on." The detective lifted his hand. "How do you know he's tall?"

"I saw him in the supermarket. He followed me around as I shopped. But when I went to pay, I didn't see him. So, I thought I'd only imagined it. I came out of the store and there he was. The same guy. Tall. Very lean. Long, scraggly dark hair. Dressed in dirty jeans and a flannel shirt. Roughed up work boots. Hadn't shaved recently."

"How tall?"

"Over six feet. About six-two, maybe six-three. I know because he's about the same height as Sam."

Skye surprised herself with the number of details that poured out of her mouth. Dark hair, thick, dark eyebrows. Dark brown eyes. Pale skin.

He had a scar near the bottom of his chin. She told Detective Munson about how she'd expected the man to have bad teeth but was surprised that his teeth looked perfect.

The forensic artist clicked away at her computer. "How was his face shaped?"

Skye paused to summon up the memory of his face as he had stood outside the store. "His face was long, thin, with a square forehead."

"Like this?" Jill showed Skye her emerging sketch on the laptop screen.

"Yes, only his cheekbones were higher and his eyes deep-set. And he had long grooves along the sides of his face. Like exaggerated dimples."

Jill nodded and made the adjustments.

"He had a bit of an accent. Kind of like someone from the south. Maybe Mississippi or Louisiana. Oh, and his hands were rough and blackened."

"Homeless type?" Munson asked.

"I don't think so. No bloodshot eyes and he had really white teeth. Like he whitened them or something. His hands had a kind of machinery smell. Gasoline, grease. Like he works on cars or other types of machinery. And besides, where would he have gotten his car if he's homeless?"

Munson nodded. "Well, some homeless people live in their cars. Stanton, run a state-wide check on stolen vehicles over the past few weeks matching the description."

The policeman nodded and left the room.

"I'm really nervous about tomorrow. The fundraising fair, I mean. I know you guys have been patrolling Our Kids more than usual. Thank you. I don't know if this is connected to the other things that have been happening to us at Our Kids, but if it is, could we have extra protection during our festivities?"

Detective Munson's eyebrows pinched. "Besides the officer who'll be roaming the crowd, we've also arranged for a K-9 and officer to be at the entrance to the fair. Sometimes, that's enough to keep a bad element from even trying to enter. And now that we have a good description of the guy that followed you, we'll make copies of Jill's rendition and hand it out to your volunteers."

Skye took a cleansing breath. "Thank you for all you're doing." She let her gaze rest on the artist's computer screen and tried not to shudder.

Detective Munson frowned. "Whoever this criminal is, we'll be looking out for him."

It was after dark, but Rocky heard the truck come back and Mr. Sam's car, too. He sneaked out of his room and slipped down the back stairs toward the kitchen.

Miss Skye sounded very upset. And Mr. Sam's voice sounded as if he was trying to comfort her.

"Another letter, left in the same spot as the first. And this one seems more threatening. 'See you tomorrow.' Oh Sam, what if this person has planned to sabotage something at the fair tomorrow?"

"We should take this down to the police station and add it to the other note.

Police? Other note? Rocky inched a bit closer.

"Yes, but what can they do with it? The note has no signature. It probably has no fingerprints, either."

Rocky heard a chair scrape across the floor. Someone had sat down, probably Miss Skye.

"How could anyone be so mean?" Now her tone sounded like she was going to cry. He hated to hear her voice like that. Usually, she was strong.

"It's hard to understand evil." Sam's voice sounded closer.

"What have I ever done to deserve this?"

Rocky heard her sob through the words. His gut clenched. He couldn't stand to hear her crying, and he still needed to hear something good. That they cared about him. Rocky came around the corner. "Miss Skye?"

Mr. Sam and Miss Skye both jumped. "Rocky, what are you doing here?" Miss Skye swiped under her eyes. "You should be in bed."

"Miss Skye, I have some really bad stuff to tell you."

"No, no. No more." Miss Skye dropped her head into her hands. "Not now, Rocky. Mr. Sam and I have other important things to discuss right now."

"But this is important."

"Did you break anything? Is one of the kids hurt?" Mr. Sam asked in his kind voice.

"No, it's not that."

Miss Skye touched his shoulder. Her eyes were

red, but the corner of her mouth quirked up. It didn't quite become a smile though. "Rocky, I'm sorry, but right now, Mr. Sam and I have to take care of other business."

Rocky made a face. He wanted Miss Skye to tell him how she loved him. "I'll wait. But this is important."

"I'm sure it is." Sam gave Rocky a comforting smile. "Tomorrow, we'll listen to your concerns, okay, buddy?" He squeezed Rocky's shoulders and then pointed him back up the steps. "I'll come up before I leave and tuck you in, okay?"

"Oh, okay." He hung his head and slowly walked upstairs to his bedroom. But he wasn't going to forget.

His heart burned with the hurt words of the dog-walker. And he hurt for poor Miss Skye.

After Sam went upstairs, Skye leaned on the table, her forehead in her hands.

Mrs. Sally hurried into the room from the

swinging door that led to the hallway. "I just spotted Sam going into Rocky's room. I take it, everything was settled at the police station?"

She knew about that? "How much do you know?"

"Here now. First things first." Sally set a cup in front of her and then pulled a warming tray from the oven. "I've made a pot of your favorite tea, and here's a serving of our lasagna."

The tea warmed her, and the meal smelled delicious. "How're the kids doing?" Skye helped herself to a bite of the pasta as the woman spooned more into another plate.

"They've all had their baths, said their prayers, and are tucked into bed. Just checked on 'em. Even little Rocky seemed asleep."

"Thanks, Sally."

Yes, the boy had seemed upset enough that he might not be able to sleep right away. Skye bit her lip. Maybe she should have heard him out. Sometimes little kids offer a kind of simple wisdom and insight to help adults with their crises.

But the thought of Rocky stole her appetite.

Sally broke into her thoughts. "When Sam

phoned and told me about what happened . . ." She shook her head and frowned. "I never thought such things could happen in Covington."

Sam came through the swinging door. "All it takes is one bad apple. I sure hope the police catch this creep soon."

"Well, I think there are more than one." Sally moved toward the hallway but paused in the doorway. "I'm glad you're back. Goodnight, you two." She cast a compassionate glance in Skye's direction before trudging upstairs to her small private bedroom.

Skye pushed her almost full plate away. "I'm really going to be glad when we're done with this fundraiser. I feel bad about not giving the kids all my attention."

"I hear you," Sam gave her an emphatic nod. "But the fair is going to be a huge success. The weather tomorrow is going to be fantastic and that'll bring out a good crowd. And the petting zoo is a nice addition."

"That's all our kids have been talking about this whole week. I love the way children can focus on the truly important stuff. Cotton candy, baby goats, getting their faces painted."

Sam grinned. "What's more important than those things?"

But when his face turned serious, Skye steeled herself. Hopefully, he wasn't going to give her more negative things she'd have to address.

"We need to keep being vigilant about Rocky, though." He stood, went to the kitchen counter, and lifted a weird-looking contraption.

"What in the world?"

"I found this underneath the big oak tree, close to the fence in the back."

"What is it?" It looked dangerous.

"It's some sort of booby trap, obviously constructed by our little warrior, innocently sleeping upstairs." Sam placed the trap on the floor, held a folded towel against his shin, then stepped on the long, flat wood. The sharp point of a stick flew forward and thwacked his shielded leg.

"Oh, my gosh, that could really hurt someone." Skye came over to examine the trap. "He really put some thought into this. Look at the little hinge that holds the stick to the wood slat."

Sam shook his head. "It's like I said. That boy

has warfare in his bones. He's got himself convinced he can hold off all attacks with his traps and weapons."

"Was that the only trap outside?"

"Nope. I went around the yard and picked up nine more of these medieval devices."

What? Skye swallowed. "Did you tell him that you found his traps?"

Sam picked up the contraption and placed it inside the sink cabinet behind the garbage can. "Not yet. I'd rather he think he's got the place surrounded. It seems to bring him comfort."

Tears welled in Skye's eyes. The little boy was trying everything he could think of to protect the people he loved. Even at nine years old, he had the soul of warrior. If she and Sam could keep channeling his protective instincts, Rocky would grow up to be a kind, strong, self-sacrificing man who could make a huge impact for the Lord.

But Rocky's traps wouldn't stop the *bad people*—whoever they were—from trying to come to the fair tomorrow. Were they attempting to mess things up and intimidate her to the point of putting Our Kids on the market? Who wanted her gone?

Who wanted to destroy her foster-care ministry?

She bowed her head as Sam wrapped her in his arms to comfort her. "Father, please keep everyone safe tomorrow. Please watch over us all. Especially the children. Amen."

Chapter Thirteen

The Ransom of Red Chief

The next day, Skye and Sam, Mac, and Aunt Connie arrived at the park around noon, three hours before the fair would open. Even though the blue sky and warmth promised a perfect day for the outdoor festivities, Skye couldn't get the tightness in her belly to go away. What if the note she'd received yesterday meant more than just another way to make her feel on edge? What if the man who'd followed and terrified her last evening had been leaving the notes? Or was he the same person who had driven by Our Kids and thrown out those Molotov cocktails? What if he showed up today and tried to do something to sabotage her event?

"Well, I'm off to help set up the decorations on the food and beverage tables," Connie announced. Even though the event happened on grass, she still wore her signature, power-red stilettos. Skye chuckled. How she admired her aunt's ability to command respect and yet also endear people to her causes.

"And I'm gonna get my paints all set up." Mac side-hugged Skye. "This is going to be so much fun."

Skye waved in the direction of both the women. "See you in an hour or two. I'm going to check on the game tables, then help Dr. Palmer organize the medical station."

Volunteers began to arrive shortly afterward. Emily had stayed at the mansion to help Mrs. Sally entertain the kids until it was time for them to walk down the hill to the park. Two more volunteers, Ashley and Dan, who attended the university, showed up to help.

Some of the band players arrived early to help set up the sound system surrounding the bandstand and Sam went over to see if they needed help. Skye headed toward the medical tent near the pen that would become the petting zoo. She veered to the side and wandered the borders of the park fenced off for the fair. Most of the fence was the six-foot variety of cyclone fencing. But there were some spots that were only four feet. Would that be a place where someone could trespass? She'd been promised an entire border of six feet. How come there were four-foot sections? And why had she not noticed it the day before when she and Mac came to set up the booths?

Well, too late to talk to the fencing company. It would be fine. The police would patrol. No need to be hyper-paranoid despite all the weird things that had happened lately.

She reached the medical tent just as a familiar short, dapper man arrived, carrying a medical bag. "Hi, Dr. Palmer." Skye greeted him and took a paper sack that he'd tucked under his arm. "Do you have anything else you need brought in?"

"Just a couple more sacks with supplies. Why don't you show me where to put this, and then we can get the other stuff?"

"Sure, Doc." Skye's stomach crunched tighter walking so close to the doctor. His words and gestures yesterday as he eyed the mansion had set up suspicions about his motives in visiting. Maybe his actions meant nothing. But how in the world did he know that she had talked about selling Our Kids? Should she just point-blank ask him? Somehow her tongue wouldn't cooperate, so she silently pushed open the entrance curtain of the only tent on the grounds that had side flaps.

The doctor laid his bag on the examining table and took the one from her. Then, reaching into his pocket, he retrieved his car keys. "Would you mind getting the rest of the things I'll need?"

He sat and fanned his face. "I think I should have hydrated a little better."

"Are you ok, Dr. Palmer? You do look overheated."

"Nothing drinking some water and sitting for a few minutes won't cure." He loosened his tie. "There are two plastic sacks in the trunk of my car. 2020 Silver Mercedes sedan."

"I'll get them, Dr. Palmer. And I'll hunt up some bottles of water, too." She took his keys, surprised that the doctor didn't even glance her way. He must've been feeling more than just over-heated.

He seemed pale and breathless. She'd have liked to ask him if he was okay, but was it proper to ask a doctor that question?

Turning without another word, she marched to the parking lot. She found the doctor's Mercedes right away and opened the trunk. Inside were two white heavy-duty plastic bags. She peeked inside one to make sure they were the correct bags. Rolls of throwaway plastic sheeting, and a roll of the thin paper they use to on top of examining tables filled it. She didn't bother to look inside the other one. Grabbing both by their handles, she moved to close the trunk, but something caught her eye. Real estate flyers. She shouldn't snoop but after the way the doctor had examined the Our Kids mansion's great room and the kitchen yesterday, what if she saw her own property listed? That was silly, since she herself hadn't listed Our Kids. And she shouldn't be suspecting the sweet Dr. Palmer, either. Even so . . .

"And you are being ridiculous," she said out loud.

Voices alerted her to a group of people emerging from a nearby car. Skye hurriedly shut the trunk and hefted the two plastic sacks. Feeling breathless herself, she hurried to deliver the supplies to the doctor.

When she returned to the medical tent, Dr. Palmer still sat there looking ill. "Dr. Palmer, I'm concerned about you. I'm going to get you some water right away, but is there anything else I can get you?"

Dr. Palmer straightened. "Water is all I need, dear. I'll be fine in a few minutes." He stood a bit shakily and approached to take the stuff from her. "I hope we won't need these, but you never know."

"I can't bring you a hot dog or hamburger too?"

"Maybe later, Skye.

Skye forced a smile, then left to perform her little act of mercy. As much as the contents of Dr. Palmer's trunk had disturbed her and awakened suspicion, she was still fond of the old man. He had not looked well. It was noble of him to come today, but it would be awful if the medical expert needed expert help himself. Skye decided to mention this to Sam and ask him to check in on the doctor regularly.

As she neared the delivery area several volunteers were hauling in crates of food. Kate Devlin's pinched, awkward smile came into view over the top of a couple of totes. "Good morning, Miss Wright." The woman seemed a little out of her element, wearing slacks and, of all things, tennis shoes.

"Can I help you?" Skye took the top tote from the stack. It wasn't really that heavy.

The woman struggled to keep her boxes balanced "I thought if I stacked the bread boxes on top of the bottles of water, I wouldn't have any trouble, but seeing over the stack was a bit of a challenge."

"Water sounds amazing right about now," Skye muttered and followed Ms. Devlin to a nearby tent. "I see you found a place to help out." She wouldn't fuss, even though the volunteers had all been vetted. What trouble could there be with someone carrying some crates of water bottles?

Ms. Devlin slid one of the water crates onto a folding table. "One of the young ladies over there almost dropped this crate. Good thing I was there to rescue her and help carry the water." She separated the boxes with bread from the crate of iced bottles of water.

"I'm glad you were there." Skye glanced

toward the truck, but it looked pretty empty at this point.

"Did you say you needed this?" Ms. Devlin turned around and held a chilled bottle out toward Skye.

"Yes, thank you. Though I could probably use a couple more." She stepped past the woman to the table and started to pull out more waters for herself and the doctor.

Kate Devlin hurried to help. " Here, I just pulled these bottles from an ice bucket. They'll be colder than the ones you're trying to get at." She handed Skye two more ice cold bottles.

How sweet of the woman. Maybe she had misjudged Ms. Devlin after all. "Thanks for your help." Skye waved one of the bottles at her as she side-stepped toward the main concession section of the fair.

"Stay hydrated." Ms. Devlin called, then held up her own bottle as if in a toast and waved as she turned to make her way toward the entrance.

Skye hurried back to the medical tent. It was good that Kate Devlin had decided to come anyway, even though she wasn't an official volunteer. Maybe she *would* offer a nice donation.

When she returned, Dr. Palmer's granddaughter, a nurse-practitioner, had arrived and was helping him set up. Good, he wouldn't be alone. She would've loved to hang around and draw out the doctor about their conversation concerning the condition of the Our Kids mansion, but voices of arriving fair attenders let her know that the event had officially begun.

She handed one of the water bottles to the doctor.

The doctor smiled a thanks and unscrewed the cap. But he paused to give the bottle a curious look. He glanced at Skye as if wanting to ask her a question, hesitated, shrugged, then he tilted the bottle and took a long drink. "Thank you, Skye."

Skye needed to attend to the front entrance next. She left Dr. Palmer and his granddaughter and hurried toward the Fair's front entrance. A nervous thrill ran through her body. As many times as she'd done these fundraisers, she never got over performer's anxiety. Would all of her volunteers do what they were supposed to do? Would all the equipment work? And would they all be safe from whoever was trying to intimidate her into selling Our Kids?

She didn't need to be at the gate when the attenders arrived, but she'd feel better if she could get an idea of the kinds of people coming for the fundraiser. Would they be families with little kids? Would there be single people? It seemed to change each year.

And what about the guy who'd scared her last night? Was he just a random weird person wanting to intimidate a woman all alone in her truck? Was there a connection—as she suspected—between the man and all the scary things that had been happening to Our Kids? Would he have the nerve to show himself today? The questions swirled about her brain like a swarm of upset bees.

She calmed her nerves and tried to be rational about all of it. To be honest, she now doubted the weird guy would show. Unless the guy was truly nuts. Besides, the police in attendance, some of her male volunteers, and one of the women were trained in martial arts. A Brazilian jiu jitsu trainer, a Karate instructor, and one former Navy Seal were ready to protect her and the kids.

No, the creepy stalker would have to be crazy to try to show up and pull off any shenanigans.

She collected a short stack of maps from one of the volunteers who passed them out and joined their task. The first group she met was a family of five. She greeted them and handed the woman a map of the fairgrounds to help them navigate around the many displays, games, and concessions.

She met a young man and his girlfriend, followed by another family. The guests all seemed eager to have some fun, nothing besides that.

Having passed out all of her maps, she moved with the crowd toward the concession area. Don, one of the concession volunteers flagged her down. "Can you fill in at the hot dog stand until Jennie returns? She had to pick up her kid at the library."

"Sure." She stepped behind the tables that held a bun warmer and a hot-dog cooker.

Sam strolled by and did a double-take just like some of those actors in old movies.

Skye handed a teenager a hot dog and a small bag of chips. "I'm filling in for Jennie for a couple of minutes. How's it going in your area?"

Sam smiled. "So far, it's going great. Ask me

the same question in an hour when the crowds start getting really big." He rounded the table and gave her a smack on the cheek.

Skye tried to cover her blush before the next patrons stepped up to order food.

He handed the couple bags of chips and took their money while Skye made up their hotdogs.

She handed them off and then turned to him. "When are the kids getting here?"

"In a bit. As soon as they arrive, I'll stay with them."

She squeezed his hand. "Thank you. What would I do without you?"

He whispered in her ear. "I don't ever plan for you to find out."

Shouts and laughter interrupted their conversation. "That must be Pastor Jim in the dunk tank." Skye shook her head and giggled. It felt good to be relaxed enough to enjoy the day. She had Sam to thank for it. His presence made her world better. "He said he'd be the first one in. By the way, could you check in on Doctor Palmer? He didn't seem well when he arrived."

The band started playing an upbeat

contemporary praise song which made it difficult to hear Sam's response. He mimed an okay sign, waved goodbye, then strode toward the medical tent near the fair's entrance.

The hotdog volunteer, Jennie, arrived, allowing Skye to continue supervising the activities. So far, so good. Fair attendees kept arriving and all the volunteers stayed busy at their various booths.

Skye spotted Mac. A little girl sat on a stool in front of her cousin. Skye moved to the other side of the girl to view the elaborate butterfly. "Ooo, pretty."

"I'm getting in the groove," Mac winked, looking even more like Aunt Connie than normal.

"Is it a butterfly?" The little girl spoke out of the other side of her mouth.

"Don't move," the woman standing behind Mac cautioned the girl.

"It's a beautiful butterfly." Skye stroked her fingertips along Mac's shoulder. "Drawn by a fabulous artist." It felt so good to have some of her family here since her parents had been unable to come.

She exited the open tent and glanced toward the

petting zoo. The animals had arrived, and kids had flocked to the enclosure they'd set up on what used to be a sand volleyball pit. The sand was perfect for the baby animals and easy on the kids as well.

And it looked like there was something else there. Maybe a clown sat inside the pen? She moved closer, but with the boards of the fence and all the people crossing her path she couldn't get a good view until she could look over the rail.

"Of all things." In the center of the enclosure, Aunt Connie was on her knees, helping a toddler feed a bottle to a baby goat. Her red dress was like a flag to the other animals, and they climbed over her legs and into her lap. She giggled when one of the lambs started licking the soles of her bare feet.

Skye took out her phone and flicked several photos. Dad wouldn't believe this. As she held the phone it vibrated in her hand and chimed. She put it to her ear and turned away from the corral. "This is Skye Wright."

"Miss Skye, this is Owen at the gate. Can you come over?"

What was this about? She assured him she was on her way and pocketed her phone. She trotted part of the way and then walked briskly toward Owen as he stood taking the tickets for entrance into the park.

"I'm so sorry for the worry," he said as she approached. "The ticket machine over there was stuck, but they were able to make it work again."

She nodded and glanced toward the lady selling the tickets. "Good job." She gave them both a thumbs up.

Problem averted. The only kind of problems she wanted to see today.

She eyed the crowd, still streaming in at a steady pace. A family with three young kids entered through the turn-style. After them, a tall man with a goatee and short coal black hair came through.

Skye's stomach went taunt. *Fraidy cat*, she scolded. Although he was tall, this guy had a slight paunch. And he couldn't have grown a beard like that in less than twenty-four hours. He grabbed a map and sauntered past her.

Skye zeroed in on his hands. Were they stained with the black stuff that came from working on engines? Argh! She couldn't get a good look. One hand was hidden behind the map. The other was stuffed in his jeans pocket. He walked directly toward the petting zoo. That seemed kind of strange. Most grown men didn't have too much interest in baby goats and lambs. Skye followed at a distance but kept her eyes on the stranger.

At the petting zoo, he lingered but seemed to watch the kids inside the pen more than the animals. A chill lifted the hair at the base of her neck. Why would a man, attending without kids, be interested in watching children? She pretended to study her own map in case he turned and noticed her.

As a teenager, she had gone to a local fair with two of her girlfriends. They'd gone on a ride she hadn't wanted to do. While she waited, a stranger had tried to strike up a conversation with her. And even when her friends rejoined her, the man had continued to follow them from ride to ride. Even now, fifteen years later, she still felt the same chill when she remembered the stranger at that fair. Was this something similar? A stranger hoping to follow a child and get him or her alone?

The thought made anger well up in her gut. How dare anyone come to a fundraiser for foster kids with the intent to lure away a child. Maybe even kidnap one. Skye sidled closer, this time looking directly at the strange man with the short, pointed beard. Maybe if he saw she'd noticed him, he'd lose his nerve and leave.

He caught the eye of a little girl feeding a lamb and smiled. Skye's anger flared. She gripped her map and closed the distance between them. But just then, a woman raised up from one of the lambs and called out, "George! Over here."

The man turned, and seeing her, smiled and waved. He hurried over to hug the woman.

The woman laughed. "See, I told you if we met by the petting zoo, we'd easily find each other. C'mon, Layla, time to get some hot dogs. A little girl raised her head, then skipped over to the couple.

Relief flooded Skye's torso while she watched the little girl leave the petting zoo and join her parents. How silly she'd been trying to play detective. She should let the professionals handle the job. And besides, she needed to get over to the refreshments booth to see if they needed more ice or lemonade.

Chapter Fourteen

Snatched

Rocky walked alongside Mrs. Sally, leading the group of children down the hill from Our Kids. He liked the walk—and being the leader—almost more than anything he'd find at the fair. It was eight downhill blocks and through a couple of parking lots. One was for people who would ride the passenger train, the one that went all the way south to Seattle. Across the street lay the train station. Buses came through there too. Then, there was the ferry building.

They'd gone there one time to look at the old pictures of how Covington looked a long time ago. He wasn't too interested in those. Looking at the big ferry and the fishing boats was way more interesting. One time, he got to see the cars loading onto the ferry. Miss Skye said it went all the way to Alaska.

He'd like to have a big fishing boat and go way out past the sound. Out onto the ocean where he could catch big fish. He'd like to see the orcas and whales.

Miss Emily and her boyfriend Mr. Mike were also walking with them. When they got to the fair, they'd all have a hot dog or hamburger and some lemonade. Most of the kids wanted to go straight over to the petting zoo after lunch. Since they all had to walk together, he'd have to go with them. Unless maybe he could join up with Mr. Sam. Then, he could go watch the pastors all get dunked in the tank. Maybe Mr. Sam would let him throw a couple of balls.

As luck would have it, Mr. Sam hung out near the hamburger stand slurping on a big glass of lemonade. "Hey, Mr. Sam, can I hang out with you after we have lunch? I don't wanna see the baby animals. I wanna be with you."

Mr. Sam handed Rocky a cup of the tangy,

sweet drink. "Why, sure. I could use your help, Rocky."

"Seriously? Me, help?" Rocky's heart soared. "What d'you want me to do?"

Mr. Sam closed his eyes as if he thought hard. Then he opened them and squinted at him. "I need to check out the generators, make sure they're all working well. They're over by the fence near the parking lot. Then, we could ask the band if they need anything."

Rocky grabbed a hamburger from the tray and squirted a bit of ketchup between the buns. "I'm ready now, Mr. Sam."

Sam let Mrs. Sally, Mike, and Emily know that Rocky would be going with him. "All right, let's take a look at the generators."

Mr. Sam kind of reached out his hand. Rocky scowled. Why didn't the grownups see that he was too big a kid to hold hands with? Then Mr. Sam lifted his hands and clapped them together. He gestured with his head, "Just follow me."

That made Rocky's chest well.

They strolled side by side to the fence edge to some machines making a loud humming noise. Sam raised his voice for Rocky to hear. "This here is the bigger generator. We're powering a couple of things with it. Then there's the generator we're using for the band. And we also . . ." His words got covered by the machine noise.

"Wow." That generator Mr. Sam pointed to had to have cost a million bucks, it was so fancy. Rocky yelled over the churning vibration. "What makes it run?"

"Well, a fluid, say gasoline, pushes some blades which are mounted on a rotor shaft. The force of the gas on the blades rotates the rotor shaft. Then the generator converts the mechanical energy of the rotor to electrical energy."

The words sounded like something out of a space movie. "And that makes it give power?"

"Exactly."

"Wow," Rocky said again and shook his head.

Mr. Sam bent over to check some things on the generator. "This one seems fine. Let's check the other one down a ways."

Rocky followed him. Off, a bit farther, people tried to throw balls into slots or toss rings onto bottles. Most of them weren't doing too good.

The other generator was smaller and quieter.

When they were done checking that generator, Mr. Sam asked the band people if they needed anything like food or water. Two of them wanted a hamburger and a couple bottles of water, so Mr. Sam and Rocky headed back to the stand to fetch all the stuff.

Rocky helped load all the food and drinks onto a tray. Mr. Don, who was running the concessions area, held up a phone and called to Mr. Sam.

"Everything all right?" Mr. Sam moved toward the man and Rocky followed. If there were bad guys here, he wanted to know about it.

"Dr. Palmer has taken sick."

"Do we need to call an ambulance?" Mr. Sam set his tray down on the table of the hotdog stand and pulled his phone from his pocket.

Mr. Don put his hand on the phone. "He'd be furious if we called 9-1-1. His daughter is hoping that he can just get a ride to the hospital."

Mr. Don didn't even seem to notice Rocky. Mr. Sam said something else that Rocky couldn't hear and then hurried off toward the parking lot.

Mr. Don picked up Mr. Sam's tray and trotted

back toward the stage. Rocky followed after him, but he dropped his stack of napkins and had to stop and collect them. He lost sight of Mr. Don, but he knew where the stage was. By the time he made it there, Mr. Don had vanished. Rocky gave his tray to one of the musicians and then looked around.

He didn't see any of the Our Kids workers, but that was fine with Rocky. Now he could do anything he wanted, and no one would tell him he had to hang out with the kids at the petting zoo.

He really wanted to get a better look at the generators again. Not that he would mess with them. All the power to the lights and the appliances came from the generators, and he didn't want to do anything that would make it stop working.

Mrs. Connie came out of a food booth. Rocky ducked behind one of the porta johns and waited until he was sure Mrs. Connie wasn't still hanging out. After a minute, he peeked out. Good, the coast was clear. He trotted in the direction of the generator. But when he got near, two men hovered over the machine. One held a flashlight and the other, a screwdriver.

Rocky spread his legs and crossed his arms.

"What're you doing?"

The two men jumped at Rocky's voice, and the tall, skinny one with the screwdriver stashed it in his back pocket. "We're trying to fix this machine. It wasn't working when we got here."

"Well, it was working a few minutes ago." Rocky put his hands on his hips and glared at the man.

"Hey kid, why don't you run along and let us take care of things." The shorter, fatter man motioned with his head for Rocky to leave. "I'm sure your mom and dad are looking for you."

"Nope. I think I'll hang out right here. Make sure you do things right."

The two men looked at each other. When they turned back to Rocky, they didn't look happy. The skinny man took a step closer. "Look, you little twerp, you need to run away before we get mad and do something you're not gonna like."

Rocky didn't back away. "Oh, yeah? At a fair, with tons of people around?"

The man dug in his pocket and raised the screwdriver over his head like he was going to hit Rocky.

Rocky jumped away, still facing both men. "I'm gonna tell Mr. Sam you're trying to hurt our generator."

He turned to run away, but the tall man grabbed him and clasped a hand over his mouth. Rocky struggled as hard as he could, but the man was too strong. The hand over his mouth made it hard to breathe. He couldn't yell, and he couldn't scream for help. The man carried him at a jog. Where were they going? He had to get free. He tried to chew the man's hand, but that made the man tighten his grip.

Rocky's heart pounded. He had to get away. But wait. How would the man sneak him out of the fair? Too many people would see them.

They were running away from the main fair area, though. At a short section of the fence, fat guy hopped up and swung his leg over it. He fell to the ground then stood up. The tall, big guy handed Rocky over the fence to him. As the fat guy steadied the fence for the taller one, Rocky got a good breath and hauled off with a yell. But it wasn't long enough. The other guy pulled him back by his shirt and clasped his hand over Rocky's mouth the same way the tall guy had done. Then tall man hoisted

Rocky back into his arms, clamped his hand over his mouth and ran across the grass, following the shorter dude to where a white work truck sat. They shoved Rocky inside onto the bench seat. Then the tall thin one scooted in and held him down as the other guy climbed behind the steering wheel and drove them down the road.

Still, Rocky couldn't scream for help 'cause the skinny guy kept him quiet. They used awful language while they drove. They were meaner than the mean man who had started living with his mom before Skye had taken him away. Wherever they were taking him, Rocky didn't have a good feeling about it.

Chapter Fifteen

Captive State

The bad guys drove for a long time. Were they still in town? Maybe they drove into the forest so they could kill him and dump him somewhere no one would find him. The thought made him struggle to remove the bad guy's hand over his mouth. But the man just tightened his grip and growled at him, like some sort of wild animal.

They didn't seem to know what to do with him, though. The tall guy said something about calling somebody that was "gonna be really mad, though."

The driver nodded. "We gotta do it, to find out how long we need to keep the boy."

How long to keep him? Rocky felt a bit better.

Maybe the bad guys weren't planning to kill him after all.

The truck slowed, took a hard turn, and crawled forward. The tall man's thigh pressed Rocky's head down so he couldn't see what was up ahead. The driver jumped out and then Rocky heard some loud cranking noises. When the man hopped back into his seat, he pulled the truck forward. The light dimmed. Rocky could make out a ceiling. A high one like on a metal building. It smelled of grease and machines. The truck made a kind of echo sound when it pulled in before the driver cut the engine.

Only after the driver shut the garage door did the tall guy take his hand off Rocky's mouth. Rocky gasped for air. "Help! Help me. Somebody, help!"

The two men both laughed. "Nobody's gonna hear you, kid. You're way far away from people".

Rocky jumped out of the truck and tried to lift the garage door, but it wouldn't budge. He pounded on it with all his strength. "Help, help!"

The men chuckled again. "Go ahead and pound. Yell all you want. Won't do no good."

Rocky stopped and looked around for another way of escape. He noticed a door on the opposite side of the building. He dashed in its direction, but the chubby man caught him and lifted him off his feet. Rocky kicked and struggled, but he got nowhere.

"Hey, Tom, get the zip-ties and do his feet."

The tall guy, Tom, opened a drawer in a big tool chest and pulled out the plastic ties. He selected a long one and wrapped it around Rocky's ankles.

"That'll hold him." Tom flashed Rocky a mean sneer and pulled out another plastic tie. "Put him down, Alphonse."

Alphonse lowered Rocky and quickly pulled his arms behind his back. Rocky immediately twisted his wrists underneath and flat against his back. Something he'd seen on a police show. It just might work.

Or not. Tom slipped the tie over Rocky's arms and pulled it tight around his wrists anyway. Then he yanked him up and carried him to the corner of the building next to the back door. He pushed him down on top of some wood pallets. "Now you sit down there and keep quiet."

Rocky wiggled to get his hands free, but it only budged a little bit. Still, he'd keep trying.

Then, the two bad guys ignored him. They both got on their phones and talked with bunches of people. Or maybe it was just one or two. Rocky couldn't tell. He examined the room. It was big. Must be a warehouse. But where? It smelled of oil and grease. And something else. He sniffed and sniffed.

Seagulls screeched nearby. Oh, it was the ocean. He couldn't be far from the water. Covington had lots of warehouses down by the water. He knew that because Mr. Sam had taken him for a drive once and told him about all the types of work men did by the water. There were fish warehouses where they got the fish ready for packing. There were warehouses that worked on different kinds of boats. Building or fixing them. And there were fabrication places. Mr. Sam had walked him down along some of the businesses so he could see and hear and smell how it was down here. And freight trains came through too.

So, that meant there were lots of people nearby. The bad guy had lied about no one being around.

Rocky made his body bounce a little on top of the pallets. "Hey, you guys, aren't you hungry? I could use a McDonald's hamburger and fries and a chocolate shake about now."

Tom and Alphonse looked at him, but they must have decided it was time to eat 'cause Alphonse went out the back door. Seconds later, Rocky heard a car motor revving.

While he waited, Rocky swiveled his wrists from side to side. Good, they began to get looser. Soon, those big losers wouldn't have a clue how easily he could escape the ties whenever he wanted. He'd keep his wrists behind his back until they both left, or went to sleep, or do whatever they were gonna do when they got tired.

Tom's cell went off and he clicked to answer. Someone was mad. Rocky couldn't hear any of the words, but Tom held the phone away from his ear while the hollering when on. Tom climbed inside the cab of the truck and closed the door. Even so, Rocky could hear Tom trying to get a word in edgewise. But he kept getting cut off by the angry caller. Tom's face was getting redder by the second. When he finally ended the call, he just sat there inside the truck, shaking his head.

Rocky did some more spying. The big room had

another door, kinda half open. It must be a bathroom. Right outside, there was a sink and a counter and a fridge. There were cupboards too. Maybe if they left him alone, he could go look inside and see if there was anything he could use to pry open the garage door.

On the other side, there were taller cabinets, and shelves that held different types of tools. There were coils of rope hanging on hooks. He gazed up at the ceiling. Yep, a couple of pulleys, probably for lifting machine parts. For sure, a boy could make all sorts of contraptions with all the things he saw. He just had to use his imagination—if he could be left alone for an hour or two.

Rocky's stomach rumbled. Alphonse must be about done getting his food at McDonald's. If he actually went there. They wouldn't let him starve, would they? If they didn't feed him, he could sure make a ruckus. They wouldn't want that, especially at night. He could make them miserable with all his hollering.

Make them miserable? Hey, maybe he just came up with a great idea. Just how miserable could one boy make Tom and Alphonse before they got annoyed enough to not think well? Before they forgot to be careful, and he found a way to escape.

The Visitor Kids Around

Chapter Sixteen

The Great Escape

Even as the sky turned dark, people came through the entrance gates. Skye could hardly believe the size of the crowd, and nobody seemed to be in a hurry to leave. The guests asked all the right questions about Our Kids and how they could help fund it. A couple of new pastors in the area had even talked to Skye about adding Our Kids to their church list of charities. So as a fundraiser, the fair seemed to be a huge success. They would know for sure tomorrow with the final accounting tally.

She glanced at the weary group of kids, some of the younger ones, clinging to Mrs. Sally. They'd had a ball getting their faces painted and feeding the little animals in the petting zoo.

As a wrap up, the music from the stage stopped, and Aunt Connie stepped to the microphone. Her romp in the sand of the petting zoo left no effects. Not a hair was out of place, and she once again wore the bright red stilettos that matched her suit. She smiled her famous smile and announced the winner of the all-expense paid weekend at her favorite resort. The audience cheered as a tired couple beamed and moved to the stage to accept their voucher.

Then, Pastor Jim took the stage. His kind voice bellowed loud and clear over the PA system as he told the crowd about Our Kids and how the community appreciated all the good the ministry did to find homes for the children, or to speed them through court battles and return them to their families.

She moved to the back of the group and scanned the area near the medical support tent where Dr. Palmer had been. Good thing his granddaughter had been there to take over when he became ill. *Dear Lord, please help Dr. Palmer feel better. Please help him to get the best treatment for whatever is making him ill.*

But where was Sam? The longer he was gone, the more she feared Dr. Palmer to be more than just a little ill. What if he had a heart attack? Oh, it could be so many bad things. Maybe she should call Sam and see if he had found anything about the doctor's status.

As if to answer her questions, Sam came around the bend and waved to her as he approached.

"How's the doctor?" she asked when he got closer.

Sam shook his head, and his face showed real concern. "When he said he'd been having shortness of breath and some mild chest pain, they scolded him for allowing me to drive him to the hospital. Said he should have called for an ambulance right away."

Skye put her hand on her chest. "Oh, my goodness. Dr. Palmer never told me he had any of those symptoms. I wish I'd known."

Sam placed both hands on her shoulders. "Well, he's in good hands now. Everybody at the hospital knows Dr. Palmer and they'll take good care of him. But since I'm not family, they wouldn't tell me anything about his condition."

Maybe she could learn about it from his granddaughter. Skye glanced toward the medical tent, but some workers were already in the process of dismantling it. The woman had probably already left. Her eyes fell on the crowd, most of them facing the stage as her kids had been earlier when she spotted them. She couldn't wait to hear all of their stories. Especially . . . "Where's Rocky?"

Sam released her shoulders. "I handed him over to Don back at the beverage area. No sense making him come along, especially if it turned into an emergency."

Worry gripped Skye's throat. "Wait, I saw Don a while back and he didn't have Rocky with him."

"Maybe he handed the boy over to Mrs. Sally or one of the other helpers."

"Mrs. Sally is right over there." Skye pointed toward the front of the stage where she'd just seen the woman. At this point, Sally stood with Aunt Connie in front of the bandstand listening to the pastor give his thoughts on helping to support Our Kids. A number of little heads stood around them both.

"Sally, Sally," Skye called.

When Sally turned, Skye came up and quickly scanned the group of kids with her. Her heart jolted. No nine-year-old boy. "Have you seen Rocky lately?"

"What's wrong?" Aunt Connie put her arm around Skye's shoulders.

Sally's face paled. "I haven't seen him since he went with Sam just after lunch. They went to look at the generators. Rocky didn't want to go to the petting zoo or have his face painted. You know how the boy is."

Skye sighed. How well she did. What mischief had that boy gotten himself into?

Sally ruffled young Alex's dark hair. "We just got here to listen to Pastor Jim's talk, then I planned to collect Rocky from Sam and walk all of them back to Our Kids." Sally's eyes shimmered. "Has the boy gone missing?"

Sam came up on the tail end of Sally's words. "Mrs. Sally, I had Rocky with me until Dr. Palmer got sick, then I handed him off to Don. Have you talked to Don in the past hour? Do you know where he is?"

Sally gave a hopeless shrug. "Last time I saw Don, he was helping out at the beverage station."

Connie stepped forward. "I helped him serve the burgers and hotdogs for a while. I assume he's still there helping Jenny."

Sam touched Skye's arm. "I'll go check with Don." He stepped backward and pointed toward her. "While I'm gone, go find Officer Stanton. We might need the police help to locate Rocky." He turned and rushed off.

Connie took Skye's arm. "I'm coming with you."

Skye's chest tightened at the thought that Rocky might have wandered off, maybe out of the park boundaries. Had he wandered uphill to Our Kids? Or did he want a closer look at the sound, so close by? Or slip onto the ferry . . . The more she wondered, the more anxiety gripped her.

Letting her imagination get away from her wasn't going to help matters. She shook off the fear and laid a hand on the older woman's shoulder. "It will be all right, Mrs. Sally. Please keep the kids right here while I find Officer Stanton."

She and Connie hurried to the north side of the

park property. They found the policeman patrolling near the empty corral that had been the petting zoo.

Skye rushed up to him, breathless. "Officer Stanton, we're trying to locate one of our boys. Rocky Cortez. He's nine years old. About this high." She held her hand to her other arm, just above her elbow.

Officer Stanton's face turned deadly serious. "Where did you last see him?"

"He was with Sam. Then Sam had to take Dr. Palmer to the hospital, so he handed Rocky off to Don Chesney, one of our volunteers."

"But after Don, we don't know where Rocky ended up," Connie added. "Sam's gone to find Don at the beverage station, but I've been with him for a good hour or so, and Rocky wasn't there."

"Can you give me a description of Rocky?"

Images of the cute little boy filled Skye's mind. "He's got dark brown hair, big dark eyes. Skinny. Weighs about sixty pounds." She pulled a packet out of her purse and thumbed through the papers that described each child in her care. "Here's his profile."

The officer took Rocky's sheet and studied the

photo. "Yes, I saw him earlier, but that was when he was with Sam. Let's get on the PA system and tell Rocky you're looking for him?"

Stanton walked with Skye until they arrived at the bandstand. "You make the announcement. I'll speak with Sam and Don."

"I'll help browse through the other stands," Aunt Connie followed the policeman back toward the lighted booths.

Skye listened to the last few words of Pastor Jim's prayer. She hurried up the steps and the pastor handed the mic over to her. "Thanks, Pastor Jim." She turned to the audience. "Thank you so much for coming tonight. I hope you've enjoyed our festivities and that you've learned some valuable information about Our Kids. We'll be concluding tonight's events in a few minutes, but before you go, I'd like to ask for your help. One of our little boys seems to have gotten separated from his group and we are trying to locate him."

Trying to keep her voice steady, she spoke slowly into the mic. "Rocky, Rocky Cortez, if you hear me, would you please come to the bandstand? Miss Skye is waiting for you here."

She gave a brief description of Rocky and asked everyone to keep an eye out for him. Fear for Rocky almost overwhelmed her, pushing out any thought of embarrassment that she had let one of her charges wander away. All that mattered was finding her little boy.

Yes, her little boy. Rocky was as precious to her as if he were her son.

When Skye finished, she motioned for the band to return to the stage and play a concluding praise song.

Families began to disperse, some carrying prizes they'd won at the game stations or munching on popcorn and cotton candy. Skye followed the families, examining every gap between people. Every short dark head. Where could Rocky have gone? Had anyone thought to check the porta-johns? She headed in that direction and began knocking on doors. All were empty except for a little girl coming out of the one on the end.

Maybe he simply found a comfortable spot inside one of the game booths or food stations to take a nap? Could it be that simple?

As much as she wanted to keep searching,

though, she stationed herself by the exit gates. Rocky might have slipped away from his group, but he wasn't leaving this park. And it would be easier for him to find her if she stayed there.

It was hard to get into the mind of a little boy, especially one so geared toward behaving independently of his caretakers. Pushing back tears, Skye smiled and said goodbye to kids and parents.

When the last groups of attendees had exited, Skye couldn't hold back anymore. "Rocky, oh, Rocky. Where are you?" The tears flowed and her shoulders shook with sobs.

Sam came up and pulled her into a comforting embrace. "Stanton has called for more officers. They're already combing the area. Don't worry, we'll find him."

She buried her face into his hard chest. His strength bolstered hers. Why had she ever thought she could do without him in her life? Her terrifying thoughts couldn't be held at bay any longer. She searched Sam's handsome face while fresh tears poured down her cheeks. "What if something bad happened to Rocky? What if he didn't just wander off. What if someone took him? You saw the note.

See you tomorrow. Maybe . . ."

"Shhh, Honey, don't think like that. We don't know anything yet. For all we know, Rocky decided to go home all by himself. One of the officers is already at Our Kids, checking it out."

Officer Stanton approached. "I talked to a guy who said he saw some unidentified men climbing over the fence near the generators. He didn't think to alert us because they were wearing work clothes, like they were there to do some mechanical work."

Sam straightened and his arm tightened around Skye's arm. "Did he give you a description?"

"It was at a distance. But he said one was tall and dark and thin, and the other was short and kind of heavy set."

Skye gasped. "Tall and thin? What if it was the same guy who tried to scare me last night?"

Officer Stanton shook his head. "Without a closer, more detailed description it'd be hard to know that. Lots of guys are tall and thin."

"You said by the generators?" Sam's voice cracked. Skye felt the muscles in his arm tighten. "Why would they be working on anything having to do with the fair. I didn't hire anyone to do that kind of work."

Skye's voice quavered. "Doesn't that seem kind of suspicious, Officer?"

Stanton's face remained still even with this new information. "We'll have to do some more investigating."

Chapter Seventeen

Clue

The bad men took off Rocky's zip binding. Just his wrists, not his ankles. He ate his McDonald's hamburger and fries quickly but took his time finishing his chocolate shake. The best part of the meal. Save it for last. That's what Miss Skye always said. Thinking of her made his heart hurt.

The sound of an approaching car almost made him spill when he jerked his head toward the one window in the warehouse. But it sat too high on the wall for Rocky to see anything.

"That's gonna be trouble." The fat man stood.

"Shut up, Alphonse." The tall man growled as he glanced over at Rocky. "Get that tie back on his wrists." Then, he went outside.

Rocky didn't say anything, just let Alphonse do the same not-good job of binding his wrists.

"Now sit down there and keep yer mouth shut or I'll stuff a rag in it." Alphonse followed Tom out the same door.

With the sound of the car engine and the sea gulls, Rocky couldn't make out anything that was said. He could barely hear their voices, and then only Tom's and Alphonse's. Whoever they were talking to was either whispering or growling.

Rocky had to see who they were talking to. If he ever got out of the warehouse, he could give the police a description of the guy. The binding around his ankles wasn't too tight. He could stand up. Maybe hop to the window. Peep outside.

He pushed himself away from the wall, inched his body farther forward. Got his feet on the floor. He tested his balance. Yes, he could hop without falling over. He made it to the window without making hardly any sound. But he couldn't see out. He needed a few inches. What could he find that he could stand on?

On the worktable next to the window was a pile

of big, thick books, like the kind he'd seen in a car parts store once when Sam took him to get spark plugs for Miss Skye's truck. One of those books, maybe two would make him tall enough to see out the window. If he could get a hold of one and put it on the floor under the window. But how?

He wriggled his hands and wrists, flexing and relaxing. There, his right hand slid partially out. More flexing and relaxing. Yep, here it came. The whole hand. He grabbed one of the big books from the table and positioned it by his feet. Argh. Now what? He couldn't hop onto the book. The zip tie tugged too tight. Rocky reached to his ankle and fiddled with the tie. He could loosen it. "Hurry, Rocky," he breathed.

There. It was loose enough. He hobbled close to the book and barely managed to step up onto it.

There was an oily grunge on the windows, but he could look through without being seen. He could only see shadows moving around in the dirty glass, but he heard Alphonse say something like "I didn't sign on for this." He sounded really upset and the widest shadow paced a few steps away before coming back.

The voices murmured for a minute or two. Then one of the thinner shadows waved his arms. Tom hollered out. "Or you'll what?"

The waving shadow moved backward. Then disappeared around the corner, probably where the car was still running.

The men would be back in a minute. Rocky hopped off the book. He had to get back to his spot by the wall. Pull the ties back on. Look totally helpless.

He made it back to his spot just in time. He didn't have time to tie his wrist but held it behind his back just like Alphonse had left him.

He heard the car screech out of the gravel lot. Whoever it was sure must be mad. A few seconds later Tom and Alphonse came back inside. They didn't say anything. Just looked angry and disappointed.

Alphonse grumbled something that sounded like, "Babysitting weren't part of the job."

Tom said, "Shut up. At least you get to go home tonight."

Alphonse grabbed a brown paper bag from off the shelf, then slammed out the side door. Seconds later, another car drove away.

Rocky managed to slip his wrist into the tie again. Then, he called out, "Hey, Tom, I gotta go."

Tom rolled his eyes. "You gonna be good?"

"Sure, I'll be good. Just get these things off my wrists." Rocky wriggled to make it clear he really needed to go. He'd check out things in there, too. Sometimes bathrooms held tools and cleaners and brushes and plungers. They might come in handy. Or maybe a window he could crawl out of if he stood on the john.

Tom took off both ties and escorted Rocky to the bathroom. But he stood there, not going away.

"Hey, can I have some privacy?"

Tom sighed. "You can close the door, but just remember I got the key." He held up a key chain and jingled it in front of Rocky's face.

Rocky smirked. "Nice to know, dude." He slammed the door and turned the lock. There were no windows in the small bathroom. Rats. Just a sink and a john. And a cabinet . . . that turned out to be unlocked.

Rocky eased the cabinet door open. Inside were the usual rolls of toilet paper, paper towels, refills for the soap dispenser. And an open box with lots of little things like tweezers, bandages, antiseptic cream, a pair of little scissors. And a big metal tray, holding more odds and ends. Hey, that might make . . .

"Yo, kid, what're you doin' in there?" Tom sounded angry. "You're taking a lot of time."

"I-I'm almost done." Rocky hurried to take care of his bathroom needs. But next time, he might take some of those little things in the box. Once he'd thought of a plan for escape.

He unlocked the door. "I'm done," he announced.

Tom didn't look impressed. "Get on back to yer place." Tom lifted a bunch of blanket-like things, except more square, from a shelf. He covered the pallets with a couple of them. Once he had tied Rocky, he covered him with the last blanket. Then, he made a bed for himself in the back of his truck.

"Time for bed. And I don't wanna hear a peep from you till it's morning."

"Sure, Tom. I'll be good." He made a fake happy face. Man, he sure would like to kick Tom. Maybe that would come later.

He curled up as best he could and closed his eyes. Tom must have flipped off the light because suddenly it was awfully dark inside the warehouse.

He hated the dark. Always slept with a night light. The wind outside made little moaning sounds and kind of brushed up against the walls. It sounded like ghosts. Rocky struggled with his wrist ties. He needed his hands free in case a ghost got inside. And he would take off his ankle tie too. The room was so dark he couldn't see what Tom was doing. Had he fallen asleep? Or was he watching to make sure Rocky was being good. Oh, he hated the dark more than Tom or Alphonse.

A tear slid down his cheek. Miss Skye always said that God saw everything. Did God see that Rocky was scared, tied up, kidnapped? Miss Skye said God really cares about everybody. Did He care about Rocky? He wanted to blubber, but he couldn't do it because Tom might hear.

"God," he whispered, "I'm scared. I know I act tough, but it's just an act. I want Miss Skye. Could you help her find me? Please help me figure a way to get away from Tom and Alphonse."

Rocky sniffled. He got his hands free of the zip-tie again and wiped his face. Then he loosened the tie around his ankle and slipped it off too. The wood pallet made a creaky sound when he tried to scuttle off it. Rocky froze and waited to hear if Tom would do anything. No, it was quiet.

The moon's rays came through the greasy window where he'd spied on the meeting. It gave him just enough light to see how he could tiptoe over to the side door and escape. Did God do that for him? Rocky decided to thank Him just in case.

Once off the pallet, he sidled over to the side door. He didn't know where he was or where he could go, but if he could get out the door, he'd get away quick. If Tom came looking for him, he could hide in the flowers and plants. They grew very tall and a boy his size could easily jump into a bush and not be seen.

He'd run all night if he needed to. Or maybe he could run inside one of those gas stations that stayed open all night. He could run inside and say, "I'm Rocky Cortez and I've been kidnapped. Please call the police." The person who worked there would call 9-1-1 and he'd be safe.

A sound came from Tom's pallet in the back of

his pickup, and Rocky froze and crouched. Listened for movement. Nothing. Just snoring. Good. Rocky kept himself low for the rest of his scary trip to the door.

He ran his sweaty hand down his jeans to dry them. Then touched the doorknob. Tried to turn the knob. It wouldn't budge. He felt all around the knob. There had to be a lock somewhere. Some locks worked when you pushed and twisted. But this knob didn't have that. Some of them had a little button on the bottom of the knob or on the side. No, no! This one must be locked with a key. And Tom had shown him he had keys.

Rocky turned back to the pallet. He wanted to kick something.

All right. It was locked, and he couldn't get out that way. He'd have to wait till morning. Maybe Alphonse would take Tom's place. He was the dumber one. Rocky could pull something on dumb-dumb Alphonse. He talked like Rocky was just a little kid, too dumb to think up a plan. But Rocky had tons of things he could plan.

Once on the pallet, he put his ties back on and covered himself with the blanket. He could lie still and plan how he could escape.

His eyes had other plans, though, closing without his say-so. He'd have to do his planning in the morning.

Chapter Eighteen

Puzzle

"Skye, you're going to make yourself sick with your fretting." Connie laid her hands gently on Skye's shoulders and held her gaze. "You've got to rest. You've been up all night."

Skye's stomach growled, reminding her she hadn't eaten since breakfast the day before. Her tongue stuck to her mouth, and she felt oh, so tired. But the thought of her little Rocky lost or wandering in a strange place made her heart quiver. There were so many dangers out there. He might have wandered too close to the water and fallen in. Or maybe some stranger lured him away with the promise of candy. And what about those workmen who came over the fence? Sam hadn't hired anyone to work during the fair. There were the volunteers and the policemen and that was all.

Aunt Connie turned her by her shoulders toward the stairs. "Now, you go get into bed. Sam's going to take Mac to the airport. And Miss Sally is going to hold down the fort. I'm going to work on your computer. Check out some of your files."

Skye opened her mouth to protest, but Connie held up an authoritarian finger. "You never know what I might turn up."

Skye turned and trudged up the stairs. She couldn't think of anything more she could do that the police weren't already doing. And she needed to sleep. As she climbed with heavy legs, she whispered the prayer she'd said so many times already. "Oh God, please keep little Rocky safe, wherever he is. Please help the police find him and bring him back to us."

After she crawled into bed, she thought she'd stare at the ceiling for hours. Maybe she'd spend the sleepless hours praying some more.

But that didn't happen. Sleep caught her somewhere in the middle of, "Dear," and, "God."

When she woke, her clock read noon. Four uninterrupted hours filled her with fresh ambition and energy, and she jumped up and quickly dressed. Tromping down the stairs, she met her aunt in the office.

"You look so much better. Did you sleep well?"

Skye nodded while combing her hair behind her ears. "Have the police called with any updates?"

"No." Connie gave her a small pout. "But I've found some interesting items in your computer folder about potential adoptive parents." She moved the monitor and scooted over.

Skye moved around the desk. "What could possibly be in them that connected to anything that's happened since yesterday?"

"Just wait until I show you." Connie used the mouse to click through screens until she stopped at one. "Now, just look at this." She opened the file. "This is a psych evaluation for a potential foster parent."

Skye's eyes widened. "How in the world did you . . .?"

"Obtain the information? Don't ask."

"Aunt Connie!" They could get into so much

trouble. "These are supposed to be private."

"We have a missing child." Connie turned to face her. "Anyway, this candidate took all the tests. But it seems her psych evaluation did not turn out so good."

"Her?" Skye spoke to so many potential foster parents and adoptive parents. Some stuck around, but most of them changed their minds for one reason or another. She couldn't think of any that struck her as needing psychological care.

Aunt Connie scrolled the mouse to the top of the evaluation and then swiveled in her seat to meet Skye's eyes. "She failed the evaluation."

Kate Devlin.

Her mind soared to her most recent interaction with the woman. "I saw her just yesterday."

Aunt Connie jerked to face her. "Doing what?"

"She was just helping to carry in some of the supplies. It was in the morning." Long before Rocky had gone missing. "The kids weren't even there yet." She couldn't have been behind Rocky's disappearance.

"She always seemed nice whenever I spoke to her." Oh, and she had seen her on Monday. The truth dawned on her.

Aunt Connie pierced her with her sharp gaze. "You've remembered something."

"I saw her at Our Kids last week right before I found the first note."

"So, she could have had something to do with it." Her aunt's voice turned harsh for a moment, then softened. "It was a childish thing to do, but it would fit with the findings of this eval."

Skye held out a palm toward the monitor. "I never saw that information. I never even got the woman's basic details."

"No, because you've been too busy working on the fundraiser. But there was enough information in your files to let me do some digging."

"It does explain why I never heard from her about fostering though. She'd seemed so excited about it."

Aunt Connie scrolled through the computer document again. "It says here that she received word that she had failed her psychological evaluation a little over two weeks ago."

Skye's mind wandered through the memories from the last week as she stared at the screen.

Clearly the notes had been left by her. But what about the vandalism? The fire had been started by a man.

And the guy at the grocery store who had scared her half to death. That couldn't have been Kate.

Then there was the weird visit from Dr. Palmer and his interest in her property. That had certainly made her suspicious. Was Kate Devlin connected to Dr. Palmer? That didn't seem possible. Then a single word from the file jumped out at her.

Realtor.

Skye pointed at it. "Dr. Palmer had a real estate brochure in his trunk. And he asked about the details of the mansion. More than just a passing interest."

Connie snapped her fingers and pointed at Skye. "I bet she's been stirring up the board to sell the house and defund Our Kids." The words from Aunt Connie's mouth would have seemed ludicrous a few minutes before they'd started this conversation. "Could the woman have had something to do with Dr. Palmer's illness?"

That question flitted past her mind, but her bigger concern was her little boy. "Or Rocky's disappearance?"

But Kate Devlin? Could she be capable of revenge because she didn't pass her evaluation? Would she blame Skye for her failure?

Skye shuddered. "Connie, I don't know what to think. This could be nothing, or it could be . . ." She paced the office floor. "I've got to think. I don't want to be hasty and jump to conclusions. It could be really serious if I made accusations based on faulty reasoning."

"Maybe we don't make accusations just yet." Connie said. "But we do need to talk to the police."

Chapter Nineteen

High Noon

Rocky had slept better than he'd thought he would. All that kidnapping junk and wiggling through the ties must have tuckered him out.

In the morning, Alphonse returned, bringing McDonald's breakfast sandwiches and a milk for Rocky. Alphonse untied Rocky and handed him his food. Rocky didn't usually eat sausage, but he reckoned it would be smart to eat as much as he could, since he didn't know how long it would take for him to find more food after he got outta there.

Tom wolfed down his sandwich, then whispered something to Alphonse. He hopped into the driver's seat of his work truck. Alphonse opened the garage bay door and Tom backed out.

Okay, so it looked like Alphonse was taking over for Tom. *Good.* The fat guy wouldn't know what hit him. It would be easier to deal with one criminal, especially Alphonse, the dumb one. How long would Tom be gone, though? Rocky needed to come up with his plan . . . fast.

By the time the sun beams streamed into the high garage windows, Rocky had studied the rope and pulley system attached to the ceiling. Judging by the chemical smells inside the building, they probably used the pulley system to lift boats or boat parts for either repair or painting. Rocky didn't know too much about boats, but he knew they needed to be inspected a lot, and they needed to have paints put on that protected the outside of the boat from water. That pulley system could probably hold a lot of things. If he could find a tray or something kind of flat, he could rig that same kind of booby trap he'd made in his bedroom at Our Kids.

There was a ladder sitting close to the side door. He'd need that for rigging his trap. He'd have to turn the pulley, so the trap was over the side door that Alphonse and Tom came in and out of.

On his next bathroom trip, he'd take a closer look at the metal tray in the cabinet. It was pretty big. Big enough to put lots of stuff on it. Heavy stuff, but small enough to fit on the tray. Things that, if they fell straight down, could really hurt your head if you were underneath. It just might work.

It had to work. He needed to get back to Our Kids and Miss Skye.

"Sir, I gotta go. Kinda urgent."

Alphonse led him over to the bathroom, but he wasn't Tom. He wouldn't let him close the door. He stood there in the doorway. No chance to look over that tray again.

After Rocky finished in the bathroom, Alphonse put the ties back on his wrists and ankles and sat him onto one of the pallets again. Rocky was bored and antsy. Well, at least he could look at all the metal parts that sat on the shelves and figure which ones would fit on the tray. Then there was the big question of how the rope on the pulley could be tied on the tray to keep it supported so it didn't fall until Rocky made it fall.

If only Alphonse would go outside so he could experiment with the tray and the rope.

"Hey, kid, you stop your fiddling," Alphonse growled.

"I'm not fiddling. Just itching."

"Well, stop it. I don't like kids. And I don't like havin' to watch a kid with the itches." He mumbled something about how "he couldn't wait for the kid to go away." Too bad he didn't say anything about how Rocky was supposed to *go away*. Or when.

Alphonse came and planted himself in front of Rocky. "I'm gonna take a nap. Are you gonna be quiet or do I hafta stuff a rag in yer mouth?"

Rocky glared up at the nitwit. "I'll be quiet."

"Good." Alphonse went over to one of the tall cabinets and pulled out an old, dirty-looking cot. The old-fashioned type that his dad used on the back porch for his naps after he'd been drinking too many beers.

The man set it up and collapsed into it with a grunt.

Rocky stayed silent and still for what had to be a whole hour. Alphonse started breathing hard, and then he started making some of the loudest, motor-sounding snores. He was a louder snorer than his dad had been, and Mom always complained about him.

He slipped out of the ties on his wrist and was about to pull the ones off his feet when a phone rang. Rocky slipped his hands behind his back and stretched out on the pallet, closing his eyes and praying that the man hadn't bothered to look his way.

"Hello."

Rocky cracked an eye open and glanced up at the man. He pushed a button and a woman's voice growled through his speaker. "Have you made up your mind yet?"

"Um." Alphonse juggled the phone and dropped it on the floor. He picked it up and put it to his ear. "Hello. Are you there?"

Rocky could hear the woman's voice rise, but he couldn't hear any of what she was saying. When Alphonse got off the phone, Rocky pretended to be asleep again.

Alphonse shuffled close enough that Rocky could smell his coffee breath, but he forced himself to lie still and let his arms and even his face go slack like a melting ice cream cone.

His nose started itching. If only the man would

leave.

Alphonse shuffled back to the cot and folded it up. Then he quieted down. Rocky dared to squint between his eyelashes.

No Alphonse.

He was nowhere in sight. Rocky wanted to get up and check the window by the side door, but what if Alphonse showed up just then?

He sat up and looked around, stretching his arms in front of him. The man wasn't there. Maybe the woman on the phone had told him to go do something. That meant, this was his best shot. He quickly undid the ankle tie. "God, I need a few minutes. Please let me do this."

He ran into the bathroom and pulled the tray out of the cabinet. The ladder was an easy set-up. He mounted the steps and turned the pulley. Yeah, these ropes would work all right. Jumping off, he fed the rope through his fingers and then tied it around one of legs of the table.

Carrying the tray, he darted over to the shelf. That tape measure would be heavy. The wrench. A couple of hammers. He grabbed enough stuff that would balance nicely on the tray. He had no idea how much the whole bunch weighed, but it sure felt heavy. If it fell on a man's head it could knock him out, for sure.

He set the filled tray on the floor and pulled all the stuff off of it. Then he moved the ladder to the door and untied the ropes. He connected the pulley like he'd done in his bedroom and then went up and down the ladder, carrying the heavy stuff a couple of things at a time until the tray was full. It would work.

It had to.

The sound of a motor startled him. No, it was two motors. One sounded like a diesel. The other was the usual sound a car made. They sounded like they pulled up together.

Rocky carried the ladder back to where it had been, then he ran back to his spot on the pallets and waited, holding the rope carefully.

As soon as anyone came through that door. Kablam!

And then he'd be free.

Rocky heard two vehicle doors open and slam shut. Then angry voices. A man's and a woman's. The man sounded like Tom. Another man started to say something, but Tom told him to shut up. That had to be Alphonse. They were close to the door. So close Rocky could understand everything they said this time.

"If you'd just done what I told you none of this would be an issue." The woman's voice sounded shrill and mean. Reminded him of the lady who had said the mean things to him the other day at Our Kids.

Tom said, "So, I should've just let the kid run back to that Sam character and tell him he saw us messing around?"

"I told you to get in there and break some equipment." This was the woman again. "Then get out. Quick and clean."

"I thought you hired me because I can think fast. Well, I thought fast. Grabbing the boy was the best choice."

"And now we've got to find a way to dispose of him. Or get him back without arousing suspicion. I've been thinking about this. Give me the kid."

Something about the way she said it sent a shiver down Rocky back.

"The heck I will." Tom's voice rose. "I know

what you're planning. You're going to take the boy back and say you rescued him. Pin it all on me and Alphonse."

Was that what she planned? Somehow, Rocky didn't quite think so.

"I said, give me the boy."

Her growl made Rocky think that he'd rather stick with Tom and Alphonse.

"Or what?" Tom didn't sound concerned, and his question was met with a moment of silence. Sounded like he'd have his way again.

But he'd still get pelted when he came in the door. Rocky stifled a giggle.

"Or I'll use this gun."

Rocky froze at the woman's words. She'd brought a gun?

The two men were silent. Maybe thinking. Maybe scared.

Tom said, "You know what? I don't give a rat's behind. Shoot me if you want but I'm getting outta here." Gravel crunched under stomping footsteps.

Tom must have been leaving 'cause right after he walked, Rocky heard the truck door creak and the motor started up.

Rocky waited to hear a gun go off, but nothing happened. She was letting Tom go. But what about Alphonse? Would she shoot him? Or would he try to run?

Then he heard Alphonse's voice. "Yer not taking the boy. I'm not gonna take the rap for kidnapping a kid."

A key in the lock jiggled the door to the warehouse. Rocky got ready. His fingers had turned sweaty, but he held the rope steady.

The door swung open. Alphonse stepped in. Rocky let the rope go. The crash that echoed in the workroom was way better than back at Our Kids. The tray and the metal pieces fell right onto Alphonse's head. The man went straight down and didn't move or make a sound.

A woman appeared at the door, gun in hand. Hey, that was the same woman who had been so mean at Our Kids.

She looked down at Alphonse, out cold, she hurried inside and grabbed Rocky before he could even try to get past her. "Come here, little boy."

Rocky struggled, but the lady was strong, and he couldn't break her grip.

"I'm trying to help you, dumb kid. Take you back home. You can trust me."

Rocky didn't believe her. Not for a second. She was mean. Had a gun. She might shoot him.

The lady dragged him past Alphonse and out into the foggy afternoon. "Let's get in the car. Everything's fine now."

No, as long as he was with this mean lady, everything was not fine. He glanced at the fancy little car. The license plate said DEVLIN 1. He'd remember that. He sure wished he had his hiking boots on. He would've stomped on this lady's high-heeled foot. But instead, he pretended to trip. And when he fell forward, his teeth clamped onto her hand like a bulldog. His bite made her howl, and she let go of him.

Rocky ran. A kid can run way faster than a lady in high heels. He ran and ran and ran.

Chapter Twenty

Revenge of the Ninja

Connie pressed the key fob to her snazzy little red convertible. "Hop in, Skye."

Skye came out of the mansion with printouts of all the pertinent information that indicated Kate Devlin's intention to foster a child, and her subsequent failure on the psychological evaluation that would keep her from following through. The evaluation was thorough and revealed anger issues and irrational rage issues that Skye would never have guessed.

Skye jumped into the passenger seat and Connie turned the car in the direction of the police station. She dialed Sam's number, but it went to voice mail. After the beep, she explained what they'd figured out. "And so now we're heading to the police station to tell all of this to the detective or someone."

"I'm sure he'll meet us there as soon as he finishes dropping Mac off." Aunt Connie patted her hand.

At the station, they requested to see Detective Munson and were directed to sit on a bench until the man was available.

"I figured we'd have to wait for a little bit."

"Yeah." The door in front of her opened and Sam walked in. Unexpected tears burned behind her eyes. Aside from knowing Rocky was okay, he was exactly who she needed right now. She rose and hurried to him.

He enveloped her in his arms. "Any word?"

"Nothing yet." She took an unwilling step backward. "We're waiting on the detective."

"Not for long." Detective Munson stepped toward them and then ushered them into a meeting room. "You'll be happy to know that Dr. Palmer is recovering. Seems contact solution somehow got into his digestive system."

"Contact solution?" Aunt Connie blew out a scoffing exhale.

"It's more dangerous than you think. It's even killed people from time to time."

"Maybe so," Aunt Connie straightened. "But who's going to drink contact solution?"

Drink. Skye gasped and the others turned to her.

"Is there something you want to tell me, Miss Wright?"

"Water. I brought Dr. Palmer water. A bottle of water."

The detective gave a slow nod. "He mentioned that all he'd had was a bottle of water. That it had been open when he received it."

A shiver danced across her shoulders. "I didn't put anything into it, Detective."

"I didn't say you did." He tilted his head. "And for the record, neither did Dr. Palmer. But I need to know where you got the bottle."

"That's just it. I got it from Kate Devlin. I said I was really thirsty, and she made it a point to give me bottles she'd had in a bucket of ice. Said they were much colder than the ones I was getting out of the crate of water bottles."

Aunt Connie stepped closer to her. "She tried to kill Dr. Palmer."

She couldn't have. Skye gave her head a quick shake. "She had no way of knowing it was for the doctor. She thought it was for me."

The detective's mouth screwed into an expression that clearly communicated his skepticism.

Aunt Connie glanced at him. "We have motive to back it up."

Skye held out the folder. "It's all in these pages we printed out. Just hear us out."

They took seats at the table and Connie hurried into her explanation. "This all started shortly after Devlin talked to Skye about her intent to foster a child. You can see there that she failed the psychological evaluation due to extreme mood swings and periods of rage."

The detective shook his head but sat across from them. "Just because someone has anger issues doesn't make her a suspect. This is a serious case and . . ."

"Detective," Skye took over, "Kate Devlin came to visit and discuss foster-care about six weeks ago. I gave her information on how to start the process of applying. But I forgot all about our visit until Aunt Connie reminded me how she showed up at Our Kids about a week ago—"

"And that was when all the weird things started happening," Connie added.

"She claimed someone had been on my porch, but there hadn't been anyone on the road. She didn't seem to have a real reason to be there, and then, right after she left, I found the first note in my petunia basket. And she'd been the one to hand me the bottle of water when I asked for it. I can't see any other way that the doctor had been . . . well, poisoned."

A knock interrupted Skye's story. A female officer poked her head inside. "Excuse me, Detective, we need you at the front."

Munson stood. "Excuse me." Without another word, he left them.

Skye met her aunt's gaze. "Do you think we're making any headway with the detective? So far, he doesn't sound very convinced by our story."

Connie opened her mouth to answer but the door popped open, and Detective Munson came inside, his dark eyes wide in amazement. "We've got the boy!"

Skye jumped from her seat. "You found him?"

"Where has he been?" Aunt Connie asked at the same time.

Skye grasped the detective's arm. "Is he okay? Can we see him? Please let me talk to him. Poor little Rocky. He must've been terrified." Tears sprung from her eyes and rolled down her cheeks.

"They just brought him in. He's been telling the officer who picked him up what happened. Seems your theory about Kate Devlin is correct."

Connie turned to Skye and pulled her into a hearty embrace. "Did you hear that? Rocky's okay."

"Let's make it brief, ladies. We'll need a lot of information from the little boy. And later, he'll need to have a complete health check to make sure he's okay."

Detective Munson led them down a corridor and through another door. When Skye saw her little Rocky, she tried all she could to keep from bursting into sobs. She needed to be strong for Rocky, to let him know she'd always be strong for him.

Rocky ran to Skye. He hugged her and wouldn't let go. "I knew you was doing all you could to find me, Miss Skye."

He looked up into Skye's face. "I told 'em. I told the police who the bad guys are. I told 'em that Tom jumped into his truck and left. And Alphonse is lying on the floor inside the warehouse. I knocked him out, Miss Skye. Just rigged it so all those heavy metal things would fall on his head. And it worked!"

Skye couldn't help but laugh. "Sam told me about your booby trap in your room. Did you make another?"

"Yep." He pulled away and straightened his spine. "But that awful lady, she tried to take me. Said she was takin' me back. But I didn't believe her. She said she was gonna spose of me. So, I got my teeth on her hand, and she screamed, and I ran."

Skye held Rocky to her and cried silently, so he wouldn't know she had broken down.

Munson had disappeared, but he came back toward them from the other side of a cubicle. "We found that guy called Alphonse. Right where you said he'd be."

Sam glanced down at Rocky and tousled his hair. "You are quite the hero, young man."

The detective chuckled as a grin spread over his

mouth. "I have a feeling Alphonse is going to have a lot to say once he's fully awake. We've put out an APB for Kate Devlin and for Tom Dunning. They won't get far."

Chapter Twenty-One

It's a Wonderful Life

That night, Skye finished reading Rocky's favorite bedtime story and set it on his nightstand. "Getting sleepy?"

Rocky sighed contentedly and snuggled into his pillow. "Miss Skye?"

"Hmm?"

"Now that those bad guys are going to jail, will they ever get out? Will they try to bother us again?"

"Well," Skye said, tucking Rocky's sheets in, "I don't know how long they'll be in jail, but I hope it's a long time. And no, I don't think they'll ever come near Our Kids again. I think they've learned their lesson."

"What lesson?" Rocky's big dark eyes opened wide.

Skye leaned over and kissed Rocky on the forehead. "The lesson for those bad guys is, don't mess with God's children."

Skye tiptoed toward his bedroom door. "Sleep tight, my little hero." She turned out the light and closed the door.

Downstairs, Sam and Aunt Connie sipped coffee. Her aunt grabbed a mug and poured some for Skye. "Well, did the little guy have anything more to say about his adventure?"

"Not really." Skye sighed. "He's still a little fearful that our terrible trio will get out of jail and come make more trouble."

"Not much hope of them getting out anytime soon." Sam came and wrapped his arm around Skye's shoulders. "Arson, kidnapping. They'll be in jail a long time."

"And what have you heard about Kate Devlin?" Connie's face filled with disapproval.

Skye almost whispered as Sam pulled out a chair for her to sit in. "She'll go away for a while. They have placed her in a mental facility getting lots of testing. At least she didn't have any part of the kidnapping. But plotting to intimidate me to the point of selling Our Kids? That's pretty awful."

"And don't forget her attempt to poison you. Good thing Dr. Palmer is stronger than he looks." Sam took a sip then put down his mug.

"He called, by the way. His granddaughter has urged him to sell his old, historic house."

"Historic?" Aunt Connie snapped her finger and pointed at the sky. "I'll be! That's why he was looking this place up and down."

"It seems he was getting pressure from her to buy a condo near her apartment so she could keep a better eye on him."

"And?" Sam cocked an eyebrow.

"He's found a small house in a senior living community, avoiding yardwork but still enjoying the freedom that he's worked for all these years."

"Another mystery solved." Aunt Connie toasted her and Sam with her coffee mug.

Sam rubbed Skye's upper arms. "It's hard to believe this was all because Devlin thought you were the one who rejected her as a candidate for being a foster care mom."

Connie sat her mug down on the table. "Can you imagine her as a foster care mother? Makes me shudder to think how she'd treat a kid living in her home. Not to mention, she ordered those two guys to try to torch your house. A house full of kids! I'm not a lawyer, but I think that'll get her at least ten years in prison."

Skye shook her head. "I feel sorry for her."

"Sorry for her?" both Sam and Connie said simultaneously.

She had a sick place in her stomach for the woman who clearly had a big empty cavern inside of her. "Yes, sorry for all the things she threw away because she let her personal feelings—misguided as they were—dictate to her all the foolish and criminal things she did. I wish Ms. Devlin had simply called me and asked what she could do in the future to qualify for being a foster care parent."

Connie tilted her head. "Unfortunately, people like her have too much pride to ask for help."

Skye sat back and flattened her hands on the tabletop. "Maybe you're right, but I still feel sorry for her."

Sam covered her hand with his. "And that's

why you make my heart melt. And it's also why I have to ask you again—right here in front of Aunt Connie.

Skye glanced over to Aunt Connie, but she had a questioning look on her face.

Mrs. Sally stepped through the swinging door. "Am I interrupting something important?" Sally asked as she filled her own mug with coffee.

Sam grinned at the woman and turned back toward Skye, "and . . . Mrs. Sally, you ladies are going to witness me in the very act of proposing to the girl I love."

Connie squealed with delight. "Now this is something I've been waiting to witness for five years."

Was this really happening? Skye's emotions did trampoline flips as Sam slipped out of his seat and knelt in front of her.

Sam continued, "Skye Wright, lovely, smart, tenderhearted, hard-working, dedicated, lover of children, and worshiper of God . . ."

He paused and pulled a box from his sweater pocket. "Precious Skye, will you marry me?"

Skye flushed as she gazed at the man. She

wasn't sure when she'd fallen in love with him, but she was sure now that it was the forever kind of love. The ring, of course, was beautiful. Leave it to Sam to find exactly what she liked. But she couldn't look at it for very long, not when Sam's dear face leaned in so close.

Now that the fundraiser had been a rousing success, and Our Kids Foster Care had received three new supporters for the ministry, Skye could focus on her own future. There was no longer any reason to delay her answer.

"Yes, my very-much loved Samuel Fortier, I will marry you."

Sally and Connie both stood up and cheered. Sam pulled Skye into his arms for a long kiss.

Connie wrapped her arms around both Sam and Skye. "Well, I guess I'll have to schedule another flight out here, that is, once you settle on a date for the wedding."

"How about a winter wedding?" Sally clasped her hands together. "Covington will look beautiful with all the lights and decorations."

"And guess who'll be in the wedding party?" Sam wiggled his eyebrows.

Skye drank in Sam's dark eyes, glistening with love and happiness, then nodded. "I agree. He'll make a handsome groomsman. Our brave little Rocky."

The *Visitor* **Has a Ball**

Preview by Betty Thomason Owens

Samantha Carr pushed open the door, and the smell almost knocked her down. What was that? Rotten eggs?

She crossed to the window and reached for the latch. It was unlocked. Odd. Mom would never leave a window unlocked. At least, not on purpose.

Mom must have been in here at some point and left the latch open. Making a mental note to remind her about it, Samantha moved to the second window and raised it.

At that moment, an engine revved outside. She peeked through the screen and noticed a man on a zero-turn mower, cutting a swath across the lawn. As he moved out of her line of vision, something on the side porch caught Samantha's notice. A large, reddish-gold dog lay in the sunshine, quite at ease, as though it belonged there.

She returned to the task at hand, determined to find the source of that revolting odor.

A bowl of something sat near the edge of the desk. The container itself was white plastic, with a green circle on the side. Samantha covered her nose and mouth with her hand. Whatever it had once been was now covered with mold and completely unrecognizable. She pulled the empty garbage bag from the can beside the desk, set the offensive thing in it and tied it off. Then she placed it in another garbage bag and tied that one. She set the doubled bag in the hall until she had finished cleaning.

Once that was gone, the smell improved a little, but she was curious. It could not have been left there by Dad. It would have been dried up by now. She shook her head to clear her mind and returned to the desk.

First things first. She gathered papers into stacks and set them carefully inside the top left drawer. At some point, she would need to go through those but not now. Time was at a premium.

Dust the furniture and vacuum.

Dad used to say that staying on task was easier if you talked your way through it. Samantha smiled at the memory of Dad mumbling to himself as he worked.

After running the vacuum, she would—wait. She stood back and examined the desk. Something was missing. A large rectangle of lighter dust on the right side of the desk confirmed it. Dad's mahogany box had stood there all her life. He had been very protective of it and always kept it locked.

Now the box was gone.

The mower outside filled the room with noise and the smell of freshly mowed grass. Samantha covered her ears. She had to think.

No, she needed to find Mom.

Enjoy The Visitor's Next Trip

Scan QR code for a direct link for purchase.

From the Story

Study Questions:

1. Skye Wright often doubts her abilities. She compares herself unfavorably to her vivacious Aunt Connie. Can you relate? What do you think God would tell Skye when she struggles with self-doubt?

2. Rocky is an unusually intelligent but strong-willed nine-year-old. If you were his foster mom, how do you think you could channel his energy and imagination so that he stays out of trouble?

3. Aunt Connie arrives shortly after trouble begins at the Our Kids mansion. If you were Skye, would you have told her right away about the vandalism and the nasty note?

4. Can you suggest some reasons why Skye is hesitating to marry Samuel right away?

5. Like Skye, have you ever experienced a perplexing, even frightening time in your life? Did you wrestle in prayer about it? How did the Lord resolve your situation?

6. Even tough little Rocky was afraid of the dark when being held prisoner in the boat repair warehouse. When you were a child, did fear lead

you to drawing closer to the Lord?

7. Aunt Connie was a strong friend and helper for Skye during the frightening times of vandalism and arson and threats. What do you think were the most helpful things Connie did for Skye?

8. Do you relate more to the confident Connie, or the sweet but self-doubting Skye?

The Unsuspecting Heather Meyers
by Shawna Robison Young

What if you've returned home to start your life over, only to discover you're there to finish it?

Ready for a fresh start, Heather Meyers flees from not-so-sunny California to her hometown in Indiana. But fate has other plans—stage IV cancer and three months to live. Determined that one more kick from life won't destroy her faith, Heather fights against its schemes. Before she can take her final rest, redemption must be found for someone she loves.

Physical therapist Dr. Jack Jones (JJ) would do anything to change the past, to not have let his high school sweetheart get away. Now that Heather's back, he'd do anything to keep her from leaving. With her time running out, he may never get his chance to set things right.

By a twist of fate and with an extra dab of this and a little bit of that, nurse Anna Ingram sets out to prove that JJ is more than his past mistakes and Heather can find hope and love in the midst of the biggest battle of her life.

Acknowledgments

Even a novella is long enough to require some expert attention from editors. Thank you, Marji Laine and Julie Cosgrove, for suggesting some truly great ideas. I truly appreciate your expertise as mystery writers.

Thank you, my patient beta readers and concept people: Kim, Kiri, Bruce, Marianne, and Jill.

Thanks to my Write Integrity Press publisher, Marji Laine, for bringing me into this fun project.

Letter to Reader:

Dear reader,

Have you ever encountered someone who didn't like you, and you didn't have a clue what you could have done to offend them? Perhaps we all have at one time in our lives.

Some people build up a perceived slight until it becomes a much greater event in their memories. The Word of God makes it clear that Christians are to overlook offences, be quick to forgive, and to not let the sun go down on their anger.

Unfortunately for Skye, she met one of the types of people who enjoy stewing in resentment, so much so that she eventually resorted to criminal activity to get revenge for a perceived offence. Something similar—but not criminal—happened to me a few years ago. A woman at my church resented my involvement in "too many ministries" there. We met and I tried to resolve the issue with tenderness and diplomacy, but without success. The memory of the difficult encounter with this bitter woman has stayed in my mind. And so, I wrote The Visitor Kids Around to help me remember how important it is to root out any bitterness before it grows and festers.

I hope you enjoyed reading about gentle Skye Wright and her struggle to trust God in her difficult circumstances. I hope you laughed at the irrepressible little Rocky and his war-like activities. I'm sure he's continuing to provide endless challenges for Skye and her new husband, Samuel.

Did you like Aunt Connie? You'll find more about her in other novellas from The Visitor series.

If you enjoyed The Visitor Kids Around, let me know. A writer always appreciates encouragement.

Here's my email: dena.netherton@gmail.com

About the Author

Dena Netherton is the president of Northwest Christian Writers Association. She is the author of seven novels and numerous short stories and articles. A frequent speaker at writers' groups, she loves to talk about the craft of writing, and  encourage them. Dena began her professional life as a classically trained musician and singer who transformed into a teacher, a musical theater director, and a Director of Children's Ministries. Her faith-filled and artistic background led easily to a life of creating compelling and suspenseful stories for Christian readers.

Also By Dena

The Hunted
3-book
Suspense Series

*How can you flee
from an unseen
enemy?*

A stalker haunts a
young woman in the
thick wilderness of the
Northwest.

Thank you
for reading our books!

Please consider leaving a review for the author
on the purchase page for this book.

Look for other books
published by

P

Pursued Books
an imprint of

W

Write Integrity Press
www.WriteIntegrity.com